I0579564

HIS TROUBLE IN TALLULAH

CATHRYN FOX

COPYRIGHT

Copyright 2017 by Cathryn Fox
Published by Cathryn Fox
Cover Design Jan Meredith
Formerly published with Samhain Publishing

ALL RIGHTS RESERVED. Without limiting the rights under copyright reserved above, no part of this publication may be reproduced, stored in or introduced into a retrieval system, or transmitted, in any form, or by any means (electronic, mechanical, photocopying, recording, or otherwise) without the prior written permission of both the copyright owner and the above publisher of this book.

This is a work of fiction. Names, characters, places, brands, media, and incidents are either the product of the author's imagination or are used fictitiously. The author acknowledges the trademarked status and trademark owners of various products referenced in this work of fiction, which have been used without permission. The publication/use of these trademarks is not authorized, associated with, or sponsored by the trademark owners.

This e-book is licensed for your personal enjoyment only. This e-book may not be re-sold or given away to other people. If you would like to share this book with another person, please purchase an additional copy for each recipient. If you're reading this book and did not purchase it, or it was not purchased for your use only, then please return to your favorite e-book retailer and purchase your own copy. Thank you for respecting the hard work of this author.

Discover other titles by Cathryn Fox at www.cathrynfox.com. Please sign up for Cathryn's Newsletter for freebies, ebooks, news and contests:
https://app.mailerlite.com/webforms/landing/c1f8n1

ISBN 978-1-928056-56-0
Print ISBN 978-1-928056-73-7

1

Former army Security Specialist Garrett Andersen wasn't sure which he disliked more, flying in small, overstuffed airplanes or attending big, over-the-top weddings. This, of course, made him wonder why he was boarding a plane at the Austin airport and heading to Tallulah, Louisiana, for just such an event. But it wasn't every day his kid sister got married, and he wasn't about to rescind on the promise he'd made to walk her down the aisle.

Knowing he was running late, he hurried onto the fully loaded aircraft and pulled the buds from his ears as the flight attendant rushed him along, closing the overhead bins behind him.

Sucking in a breath, Garrett twisted sideways and walked down the narrow aisle in search of his row. He briefly paused to help a harried woman secure her bag in the overhead compartment while her young son bounced excitedly in his seat.

Garrett cast the rambunctious child a curious glance in time to see him pull a wad of pink bubblegum the size of a shooter marble from his mouth. He wrapped it around his thumb and forefinger, then shoved it back in again, all the while climbing the headrest and playing peek-a-boo with the elderly man and woman behind him.

The mother gave Garrett an apologetic look. "It's his first time flying and I'm just trying to keep him pacified."

"It seems like you're off to a good start," Garrett assured her.

The boy continued to jump in his seat, gaining momentum with each lunge. On his descent his foot slipped and he came down hard, hitting the firm headrest stomach first. The huge ball of gum shot from his mouth and landed with an undignified splat on the man's lap. The boy blinked a few times, then let loose an ungodly howl, sharing his outrage at full volume.

"Or maybe not," Garrett retracted.

Panicked, the woman rifled through her purse for more gum, only to come up empty handed. Garrett grimaced as the shrill sound cut like a blade, and snatched a new blister pack from his rucksack, partly to pacify the kid and partly for his own self-preservation. He quickly handed it to the woman as all eyes turned their way.

"Don't worry, pal," Garrett said, scrubbing his hand over the boy's head. "We'll have you back to blowing bubbles in no time."

The kid's mom gave Garrett a grateful smile before he continued up the aisle, happy to find his section of the craft kid-free. Even though children weren't in his future, it wasn't like he had anything against them. It was just that after last night's meeting with his boss and other members of the Security Committee, a hyper kid with a penchant for big gobs of gum was a distraction he didn't need. Not when his game plan for this flight was to figure out a way to convince the Committee he had what it took to head up the new security alarm response team in Austin's business district.

Emotionally damaged my ass.

His hand went to the scar on his face, and that's when he noticed the gorgeous stranger in the window seat—*his* window seat. He gave a slow shake of his head, not at all surprised by to find a woman claiming his spot. After all, he knew firsthand that beautiful women played by their own rules. Then again, it wasn't like he had a problem with their conduct, considering he was happy to play their game. At least that way everyone walked away satisfied. And Garrett Andersen, ex-soldier turned corporate security specialist, *always* walked away.

Her sweet scent filled his nostrils, and his cock twitched in response, the enticing aroma garnering his attention while erotic images flashed in his mind's eye. He took a moment to peruse the woman next to him. His glance drifted over the sunshine-yellow strappy dress that showcased a slim frame and killer legs he'd do just about anything to feel wrapped around him. His glance traveled back to her pretty face, and he couldn't help but wonder how those long, loose curls of hers would feel on his skin, or look spread across his pillowcase.

As he considered the sensual image a moment longer, his game plan instantly headed south. No surprise really. After all, he was a red-blooded male and this sexy beauty was a distraction any guy would be crazy to ignore.

Big brown honey-flecked eyes that looked stark against pale skin and chestnut hair darted to his and then flicked back to the ground outside.

Despite his aversion to the aisle seat, Garrett secured his rucksack in the overhead bin and dropped down next to her. He reached for his belt, his hand accidently brushing her leg. She recoiled, her eyes wide and troubled as they flashed back to his. Okay, so flinching wasn't quite the reaction he'd hoped for.

He was about to introduce himself when he noticed the way she shifted restlessly in her seat, and that's when understanding hit harder than the hot blast of flying shrapnel.

Appearing more panicked with each second, her entire body tightened as if under assault, and something in the anxious way she tented her fingers seemed so familiar to him. Garrett turned to her, and held his hand out in an attempt to pull her attention away from take off.

"I'm Garrett."

She hesitated for a moment, then slipped her hand in his. His fingers closed around her hand, swallowing it whole. "Tallulah," she returned. There was a hitch in her voice when she rambled on with, "But my close friends call me Lu, or Lula and sometimes even Lala."

"So, Tallulah," he said, holding her hand longer than necessary, "it's nice to meet you."

After a long moment, he released her hand and she pulled it back to her lap. Unease registered on her face as she smoothed her dress over her thighs. "I didn't mean to suggest...I know we're not close friends or anything, and I'm not suggesting that we should be," she said, her attention on him as she fumbled over her words. "I mean, it's just that we're going to be sitting together for hours...I was only trying to say..."

The plane taxied down the runway and in an effort to keep her focus off takeoff, Garrett held his hands up, palms out. "Whoa, hang on there, Tallulah. We just met. Stop trying to rush things along between us. Heck, the next thing I know you'll be trying to get me to join the mile-high club with you."

She opened her mouth, but Garrett gave her a wink and cut her off. "And just for the record," he added raising his voice to be heard over the roar of the engine as the plane skyrocketed, "just because I gave my seat up to you, doesn't mean I'm going to give anything else up."

Eyes full of genuine shock shot to the overhead seat numbers, and a soft pink flush crawled up her long neck as scrabbling fingers went to her belt.

Garrett sat in stunned silence, because he fully expected this beautiful woman to come back with some smart-ass comment, not, "I...I'm so sorry...I didn't know. I never meant to take your seat. I don't know what I was thinking." She gave a hard shake of her head and her fragrant hair flared around creamy shoulders. The floral scent of her shampoo filled his senses as she finished with, "I guess I've just been preoccupied with other things."

Aww shit...

He sat quiet for a long moment, feeling like a world-class prick for embarrassing her. When the plane finally began to level off she unhooked her seatbelt.

"I'll switch with you."

He closed his hand over hers to stop her, then snapped her belt back into place. "No, wait. It's fine. I was just trying to..." He stopped, not wanting to mention the words "take-off", otherwise she might start panicking again.

"You were just what?" she asked, the honesty in those big eyes of hers catching him off guard. Christ, was she for real? He wracked his brain, unable to remember the last time he'd seen a woman blush, if ever, or the last time he'd come across a woman who was as sweet as she was sexy.

"Nothing, it's just..." He exhaled slowly and shook his head. "Maybe we should start again." He extended his hand and smiled. "I'm Garrett Andersen."

She slipped hers into his. "I'm Lu, but you can call me Tallulah Duncan."

Garrett laughed, and a smiled pulled at Tallulah's lips. Sweet, sexy *and* funny. The perfect trifecta.

"So, Tallulah Duncan," he began, once again noting that there was something about her that seemed so familiar. Now that the plane had leveled out and she seemed more relaxed, he put his mouth close to her ear, filling his lungs with her arousing scent. "What's so important in Louisiana that you'd subject yourself to flying when you hate it so much?"

His breath washed over the long column of her neck and he felt a shudder move through her. She cleared her throat. "I don't hate flying."

"Oh yeah? You could have fooled me."

Shifting closer, he crowded her, his body craving intimacy even though she was all kinds of wrong for him. Everything in the way she talked, moved, looked around with bright-eyed innocence screamed that she was a forever kind of girl—far different than the women he normally associated with. The last thing he wanted was a wife and family. He'd only end up letting them down.

She sucked in a tight breath, her small breasts rising and falling in the most mind-fucking ways. His body stiffened and his thoughts raced, sorting through all the things he could do to relax her.

"It's not the flying. It's the wedding."

Whoa.

Garrett pulled back and glanced at her ring finger. "The wedding. You mean—?"

She gave a quick shake of her head. "No, not me. My brother."

"Ah," Garrett said, finally clueing in as to why her gestures seemed so familiar. "Let me guess. Your brother is Ving Duncan."

"How do you know that?"

"Because he's marrying my sister, Jenny."

Garrett watched as understanding dawned in her eyes. "You're *that* Garrett Andersen?" she asked, her eyes wide, her mouth hanging open. "The one who served overseas with my brother?"

"The one and only."

"I've heard Ving talk about you."

Garrett tugged on his T-shirt collar and inched back to put a measure of distance between them. "He talks about you too. But he calls you Tally, which is why it took me a minute to figure out who you were."

A warm smile came over her face and it was easy to tell how much she adored her older brother. "He's the only one who calls me that."

The flight attendant came by and Garrett accepted a cup of water. He drank it down, but it did little to cool his heated libido. Thank Christ he found out who she was before he really turned up the heat. Unlike Ving, he wasn't the settling down kind, and if his comrade knew he was interested in his sister, his intentions less than honorable, fly boy would hand him his ass back on the blade of his Apache.

"I can't believe we haven't met before this."

He stuck his plastic cup in the magazine holder in front of him. "Yeah, what are the odds?"

"Well, Ving and Jenny did have a bit of a whirlwind romance," Tallulah said.

He looked at her a moment longer, and wished he'd paid more attention when Ving talked about her. The one thing he did remember his comrade saying was that she was a small town girl—sweet and naive—and he wanted to keep her that way.

"So Tallulah, huh?"

She nodded, like the question was one she was asked often. "I was adopted, and all the paperwork had Tallulah written across the top. Obviously because that's where my adoptive parents lived, and where I was going," she went on to explain. Then with a resigned shoulder roll she added, "So it just sort of stuck."

"Well I'm glad, because I think it suits you."

She arched a brow. "You think being named after an old railroad water stop suits me?"

Garrett laughed. "And your brother?"

She leaned into him and he tried not to stare at the dip in her cleavage or note the way his body reacted to her heat. But he was a man. And he was weak. So he looked.

In a conspiratorial voice, she said, "Well Ving is short for Irving. Irving, Texas. That's where our folks lived before moving to Tallulah. But he hates it, so you didn't hear that from me."

"I guess you two should be thankful that your folks weren't from Bullfrog, Arkansas, or Barney, Georgia, when they adopted."

She laughed, and as the sweet sound settled deep in his groin, he wondered if that sexy voice of hers would drop an octave during pillow talk. Not that he should be wondering about such things. Not with her, especially after finding out who she was. But damned if he could help himself.

"I was always partial to Peach, Pennsylvania," she added.

Enjoying their easy banter and the intimate way she confided in him, Garrett settled deeper into his seat and contemplated her other secrets. "Peaches it is, then." He had no doubt that she would taste as sweet—everywhere. "So, Peaches," he teased. "I'm really looking forward to meeting these creative parents of yours."

At the mention of her parents apprehension returned and once again she began tenting and un-tenting her fingers.

Garrett's glance moved over her face. "I hope you don't play poker." When she gave him a confused look, he nodded toward her hands. "You're an easy read." She parted her hands, and nodded her head in agreement. "You want to tell me about it?" he asked.

A noise sounded in her throat. "Not really."

Garrett scanned her face a second time. A barrage of

mixed emotions swam in her almost-too-big brown eyes. "Let me guess, your brother is getting married, and now your folks are going to be pestering you, wondering when you're going to be walking down the aisle."

"Pretty perceptive, aren't you?"

"So I'm right?"

"Yeah, but that's not all."

He gave a mock shiver. "Isn't that enough?"

Her small hand closed over her stomach, her eyes widening with interest as she watched his reaction. "It's just that, well, they're very protective of me."

"And?" he probed.

"They didn't want me to move. But after college I wanted to get away. My brother was in Austin so I moved there. Then I got at a job at a daycare, with lots of room for advancement."

He nodded. "It's a big city. You're their baby girl. I get it."

"And when my ex insisted that if I was still single when I came back, we'd get engaged, I agreed." She groaned inwardly. "I didn't want to rock the boat, and my parents only gave me their blessing to go because they figured with Jason waiting at home for me, I'd eventually come back and reunite with him. Honestly, everyone believes we're as good as married and now they're expecting an engagement announcement." She buried her face in her hands. "It was a stupid thing to do."

He let loose a long whistle. "Oh, yeah. Damn stupid."

"Hey." She shot daggers at him. "You don't have to agree with me."

"So what are you going to do now?"

She pursed her lips for a moment then crinkled her nose before saying, "I was thinking of fibbing and telling them I'm engaged."

He gave a slow nod of his head as the full picture of

Tallulah Duncan formed in his mind's eyes. "Because the truth is harder and you don't want to hurt anyone?"

"Yeah. They all think they know what's best for me."

God, she really was sweet. The women he knew cared little about other people's feelings. Their thoughts and actions were always self-fulfilling. "Do they?"

She glanced out the window, and once again he noticed her touching her stomach. "I don't know. Maybe I should just do it."

Garrett frowned as he watched her and something strange tightened inside him. Christ, he barely knew this girl, yet everything in his gut wanted to care. Fuck. "You don't want to do that."

Her voice was soft, hushed when she said, "I know."

She stayed quiet, too quiet, and Garrett touched her chin and turned her back to face him. The second those worried, honey-flecked eyes met his, it completely disarmed him, bringing out the protector in him. But he knew better than to step into that role.

"So what will you do when they start asking about him?" he probed. "Wanting to know all the details about this phantom fiancé of yours?"

"I'll make it up. Then when I return to Austin I'll tell them it didn't work out."

Garrett shook his head. "You'll never pull it off."

"How do you know?"

Because he was a specialist. An expert. A hard-core military man trained to read people. His hand went to the scar on his cheek. At least he used to be.

"Because I do," he said, offering no further explanation.

He took a moment to give her dilemma further consideration. As he mulled it over, a crazy idea hit, his mind finding a solution—for both of them. She needed a fiancé and he needed to show the Committee he was their guy. What better way to prove that he was emotionally stable than to have a fiancée—a sweet and sexy daycare teacher nonetheless—by his side.

Tallulah let loose a long, slow breath and pinched the bridge of her nose. "I have no idea why I'm telling you all this."

"I do." Garrett thought of his time overseas with Ving and how they were always pulling pranks on each other to help loosen the tension. As he thought of the fake snake he'd put in his friend's rucksack, one that damn near sent his comrade over the edge, he couldn't help but chuckle. This half-cocked scheme he was currently cooking up might actually prove to be fun, as long as behind bedroom doors he kept things platonic—the last thing he wanted was for a sweet thing like her to get under his skin—then they'd both get want they wanted, and walk away satisfied.

"You do?" she asked.

"Yeah." He pulled the tight silver band off his pinky and placed it onto her left index finger. "Because I'm your fiancé, that's why."

Dumbfounded, Tallulah stared at Garrett, hardly able to believe what he was suggesting.

"So what do you think?" he asked. "Are you up to pretending we're engaged for the next month or so?"

"I don't know." She turned to look out the window, trying to wrap her brain around this unexpected turn of events. "This is all coming at me rather fast."

"But you do think it will work, don't you?"

She shook her head. *Was he for real?* "You can't be serious."

"Why not? It will get your ex off your back and give your parents the engagement they wanted."

She turned back to him and all teasing was gone from his

expression. She took in his dark hair, slightly longer than military standards, and sapphire-blue eyes as they stared at her, waiting for her answer. Her gaze moved to the crescent scar running along his right cheek, but it did little to distract from his good looks. In fact it made him looked rugged, sexy, a man who'd go to battle for what he believed in.

"Because I don't even know you," she said.

He glanced at his watch. "We have time."

"My brother..."

Garrett screwed up his handsome face, and it made him look so damn cute she nearly swooned. Thank God she was buckled in, otherwise she feared she'd drop to the floor, or float to the ceiling.

"Yeah, I know he's going to kick my ass. But if we can convince him we're madly in love then he'll back off." He squared his shoulders. "And if not, I'm pretty sure I can handle a beating." He snorted, and a grin curled his lips like was remembering something from the past. "He probably owes me one anyway. Besides, when this is all over and we tell him the truth, we'll all have a good laugh over it. In the meantime we can have some fun with him."

"And how do you suggest we convince him we're in love?"

He shifted closer, and the warm heat of his body wrapped around her in the most enticing ways. She tried not to stare at those broad shoulders and hard body of his, but by God, she was only human, and this guy had hot, thigh-melting sex written all over him. Not that she'd ever indulged in that kind of sex before. No, her experiences weren't anything to write home about. They were clumsy and awkward and something she endured, not enjoyed. But she'd read about hot sex before, and damned if she didn't want to experience it. Just once.

Too bad she wasn't a one-night-stand kind of girl. Her hand went to her stomach. If she was, then she never would have considered following through with the pact she'd made with her ex—a pact that would lead to a quick marriage and possibly give her the one thing in life that she really wanted before it was too late.

"I guess the first thing you should do is try not to flinch when I touch you."

Oh, Gawd...

"You're going to touch me?" she croaked out.

That bad-boy grin on his face tightened her nipples. "Oh yeah, lots."

Her pulse leapt as she thought about this guy touching her for the next few days, months even, with those huge work-roughened hands. She envisioned his palms sliding over her bare skin and pleasuring her in ways she'd only ever dreamed about.

"Tallulah," he said, pitching his voice low. "Are you okay?"

"Yes," she lied, trying for calm as she forced that one word past her lips. "So this touching, what will it involve?" she questioned, far more intrigued than she really should be, seeing as this was just a ruse and he had trouble written all over him.

"When we're in public we'll have to be touching all the time. You know, to convince everyone we're lovers."

"And when we're not?"

"Then I'm afraid you'll have to try to restrain yourself," he teased with a smirk. "You'll have to keep your hands to yourself behind closed doors."

"That shouldn't be a problem," she lied. "You're not my type."

Ignoring her comment—and no doubt seeing right through it—Garrett took her hand in his and ran his finger over the inside of her arm. A warm shudder moved through her.

"That's a good start," he murmured.

"What?" she asked, her thoughts fragmenting as her skin came alive beneath his fingers.

"You didn't flinch. In fact, you almost made me believe you liked it."

"I...uh...just trying to do my part," she said as his glance dropped to her mouth.

"Tallulah," he murmured as she moistened her lips.

"Yeah?"

"I think you should touch me."

Her eyes slid over his chest. "And here you accuse me of trying to rush things along," she mumbled under her breath.

He grinned and placed her hand on his chest. She could feel the rhythmic beating of his strong heart beneath a layer of packed muscles. As though moving of their own accord, her hand trailed lower, taking pleasure in his hardness and the rippling waves along his washboard stomach. She stopped before she reached the buckle on his jeans, even though her fingers itched to go lower, to discover if he was just as hard...everywhere.

A low groan crawled out of his throat, the heat between them tremendous when she pulled her hand back and murmured, "That's good, Garrett. Very convincing."

"High school drama club," he said without missing a beat and moved closer. As he pressed his arm and leg against hers in scintillating ways, everything inside her urged her to step out of character, to throw caution to the wind and have her wicked way with him. "Oh, and there'll have to be kissing. Lots of kissing."

She swallowed.

"We should probably practice that too," he suggested.

While she sat there trying to wrap her brain around what he was suggesting, he dipped his head, his mouth hovering close.

"But—"

"You do want to get this right, don't you?"

"Yes, but—"

Before she could finish, his lips closed over hers, taking full possession of her mouth. Heat thrummed through her bloodstream and, despite her better judgment, she found herself opening for him, welcoming the kiss and all he had to offer. Somewhere in the back of her mind she registered his soft moan, the increased pressure on her lips and the blazing fire licking over her thighs.

His tongue slipped inside to play with hers, and tension grew in her body, her heart racing wildly. One hand gently cupped her face and everything in the way he held her felt deeply intimate, highly erotic. Her body quivered, beckoning so much more from this hot, heroic soldier, a guy who went to war for his country and all the people in it.

The fresh scent of his recently showered skin curled around her, fueling her hunger in the most frightening ways. If the man kissed this good, she could only imagine how skilled he'd be between the sheets. And imagine she did...

A moment later Garrett eased away and she found herself leaning toward him as he inched back. Then she drew a ragged breath, forcing oxygen back into her brain before she did something she might regret later, something like ask him to initiate her into the mile high club.

"Another good start," he said, running his tongue over his bottom lip as though savoring the taste of her.

"Garrett?" she asked, barely able to string together a coherent sentence.

"Yeah?"

"Why would you do this for me?"

He pushed deeper in to his seat and once again offered her that sexy lopsided smile that nearly turned her inside out. "Because I need a favor too."

"Ah, I get it. You scratch my back and I'll scratch yours."

His grin widened, and his voice came out a little deeper when he said, "Sure. If that's what you want."

Want? Good God, he had no idea... Then again, he was a man of experience, so maybe he did.

"What I want to know is what I have to do in return."

"Pretty much the same as we'll be doing during the wedding. When we get back to Austin, I'll need you pretend to be my fiancée in order to lock down a security job I'm vying for. I'm in competition with a guy named Phillip McNeil. He's a stand-up guy, married, kids, the whole package. The kind of character the Committee is looking for."

"What will we have to do?"

"We'll have to attend a few dinners where you'll meet the Security Committee in charge of putting together the new team, and help me convince them we're in love and that I'm the better candidate. Nothing too serious. Besides, I'm sure we'll have the part nailed by the time we return."

Nervous anticipation moved through her as she thought about what she was getting into with Garrett Andersen. According to her brother and a few other soldiers she'd once heard talking about him, he would protect the brotherhood at all costs, and die for any one of his comrades. She also knew he helped his comrades train service dogs and put them into the hands of soldiers who were working to defuse munitions that had been left over from former training camps during the wars. But when it came to women he was a playboy with a different set of rules. Ones that didn't involve long term.

Not that she was looking for long term from him. She wasn't. But she couldn't deny that Garrett Andersen made her think of sex—hot, wild, rattle-the-headboard kind of sex that would forever rock her world. And Lord, that kiss. It was pretty damn incredible and left her dormant libido craving so much more from him. She nibbled her lip and started to rethink this dangerous game they were playing.

Steeling herself, she pulled her hand away. "Maybe this isn't a good idea."

"It's your call, Peaches," he said, putting the ball in her court.

She took a long moment to mull things over. While she might have had a moment of weakness where her ex was concerned, understanding a quick marriage could give her the baby she always wanted—before her endometriosis got any worse and she ended up in surgery that would forever leave her barren—she knew she didn't love him or want to spend the rest of her life in a small town with preconceived notions of women's roles.

Then there were her parents. They were strict disciplinarians and she'd learned to do what was expected of her. She'd never been taught to stand up for herself and always tried to please them. Right now they wanted her to come home, because, like everyone else, they thought they knew what was best for her. But Tallulah loved her job in the city and was in line for the director's position. And as much as she hated to deceive them, this would give them the engagement they were looking for and help cement her reasons for staying in Austin. Her glance moved over Garrett, and to the way those perceptive eyes of his were watching her too carefully.

Garrett certainly wasn't the local boy they'd want to see her with, and her folks would undoubtedly praise the good Lord when she eventually told them it didn't work out. But in the meantime a pretend engagement with this seriously attractive guy would buy her some time until she really did find a fiancé. Plus, she wouldn't have to sit through a family intervention where everyone insisted it was time for her to come home and get married.

Oh, and there'll have to be kissing. Lots of kissing.

She exhaled slowly and continued to think things over. She considered her choices, and while one was less than appealing—she stole another glance at Garrett—the other held a promise of excitement. And kissing. And touching.

At least in public.

"Okay, Garrett." Good God, she could hardly believe what she was about to do as she checked her watch. "Tell me everything. Starting with where you were born."

2

A half hour before landing Garrett and Tallulah pretty much knew all the basics about each other's lives, all except the intimate details. But as long as he stuck to the plan behind closed doors—and he had every intention of keeping his distance with this sweet and innocent forever kind of girl—those private particulars would always remain a secret. He did, however, learn about her childhood and her best friend, Kat Stiller, who she couldn't wait to see. He also learned about her few failed relationships, and the director's job at the day care that she'd been coveting and working her butt off for. And oddly enough he'd come to realize that they both attended the same health club, and on the weekends she taught dance to the young and water aerobics to the old.

"So I'm thinking that just about covers it," Tallulah said, drawing a feeling breath and taking a drink of water after their long flight and even longer conversation. "Hopefully we can just wing the rest."

"There is one more thing I want to know" With curiosity getting the better of him, his gaze moved over her face.

"Oh, what's that?"

"Why were you thinking of doing it?"

She frowned, because she knew exactly what he meant. "It's a long story."

Even though he was treading on personal boundaries, and he'd just lectured himself on keeping his distance, he said, "We still have time."

A long pause, then a pained expression crossed her face. "I want a baby more than anything in the world."

"Oh," he said for lack of anything else because he hadn't seen that coming. "And you want to have this baby with your ex?"

"No, not really," she murmured, then tossed her arms up in the air and gave a resigned sigh. "I guess you know everything else about me so you might as well know this too." Her glance met his and she went on to explain, "You see, Garrett, I have endometriosis and two days ago the doctor told me that with every passing day my chances of conceiving are getting slimmer and slimmer." She shrugged. "Jason's a good guy, and I suspect he'll be a good father. Chances of meeting someone, falling in love, getting married and conceiving in the next few months are pretty slim, so I just thought..."

"What about adoption?" he suggested, knowing she was adopted herself.

"I'm a twenty-five-year-old single woman. Not a great candidate."

Garrett considered that a moment longer. "What about artificial insemination?"

"It's expensive and doesn't always work." She became quiet, thoughtful for a moment. "Plus, I really want my baby to know its biological father. Maybe it's because I never knew mine." She shrugged, and added, "I guess that's important to me."

"I can understand that."

"Then there's the fact that my parents don't believe in artificial insemination. They're extremely religious."

He nodded, knowing from his sister, Jenny that her soon-to-be in-laws were old school and deeply involved in the Catholic church. Which was one of the reasons they were having the wedding in the town's century-old cathedral, the same one Tallulah's parents had been attending for the last twenty-five years. Since it was only him, his sister and mother —and a handful of others, including Ving's fellow comrades and a few of Jenny's closest friends, it was much easier for them to fly to Louisiana for the wedding than for Ving's huge, close-knit family to fly to Texas.

Then another thought hit and his chest tightened. While he was happy to help Tallulah out in the fiancé department, there were some things he just couldn't do, and he needed her to be clear on that before they went any further.

He shifted, uncomfortable. "Listen, Tallulah about this baby. I can't help you out with that. I'm not cut out to be a dad."

Curious eyes met his. "Don't worry, Garrett, I'm not looking for anything more than a pretend fiancé. And besides," she said, her voice breezy, like she was trying to lighten his suddenly somber mood, "you already warned me to keep my hands to myself behind closed doors."

He attempted a smile, thankful that she hadn't probed deeper into his personal life, and they both knew where each other stood on the matter of children. "Just for the record," he said, "I think you'd be a great mother." With that he sank back in his seat and prepared for landing.

A short while later, they exited the plane and made their way to the luggage carousel. As Tallulah stood there, her nervous glance darting around all the people milling about, he slipped his arm around her waist, stepping into the role of adoring fiancé. He felt her tighten at first contact, then she sagged into him and waved to her brother from across the airport as he stared at the two with equal measures of confusion and anger.

A scowl came over Ving's face. "Garrett," she murmured, her voice unsure.

"It'll be fine." He gave a reassuring squeeze. "If we can convince our siblings, then we can convince anyone."

Just then he saw Jenny coming from the washroom. She hurried to catch up to her fiancé, who was storming their way.

"Show time," Garrett said, putting on his best charming face.

"What the fuck do you think you're doing?" Ving asked, his glance bobbing back and forth between the two as he approached. In a familiar fashion he tented his fingers, cracking each knuckle in the process.

"Garrett," Jenny cried, and pushed past Ving to give her big brother a hug. "I'm so glad you're here."

Garrett let go of Tallulah, and returned Jenny's hug. "I wouldn't miss it for the world, kiddo."

She whacked him and gave a playful roll of sapphire-blue eyes that mirrored his. "Yeah, because I know how much you love weddings and believe in happily-ever-after."

He grinned, not bothering to correct her. But truthfully, it wasn't that he didn't believe in happily-ever-after. He just knew he could never be the guy a family needed him to be and he'd eventually let them down, the same way he'd let down everyone he'd ever cared for: his mother, his father, his sister, the family in Afghanistan. The army might have discharged him a hero, but he knew he was anything but.

"Which brings me back to my question," Ving said, pulling Garrett's attention back as he took a threatening step toward him. "What the fuck is going on?"

Jenny's eyes widened and she placed her hand on Ving's chest. "What's the matter with you?"

Ving looked at Jenny and his dark eyes softened. Garrett felt his heart pinch. There was no doubt that while his comrade was as tough as nails, he was a big pushover when it came to Jenny. "Your brother here had his arm around Tally."

Jenny spun around, her long, dark ponytail swinging wildly. "What? Really? What's going on?"

Garrett once again pulled Tallulah close and Ving snarled. Keeping the grin from his face, Garrett curled his arm around her shoulders and anchored her to his body in a show of possession. His pretend fiancée blinked up at him and when he saw something briefly move over those eyes of her—something that resembled heat—it took all his effort not to drag her to the nearest hotel to sate his need to taste her.

Jenny's eyes widened in delight as she watched the exchange. "You mean you two? Are you kidding me? When? How?" She whacked her brother again, her bony knuckles digging into his biceps. "Why didn't you tell me?"

Garrett's mind raced for a plausible explanation, but without missing a beat Tallulah came to his rescue. "Because you were going through your own whirlwind romance and this week is about you, not us."

Jesus, Tallulah might be an easy read, but when push came to shove she was quick on her feet and good with her words, making up for her misgivings. Damned if he wasn't impressed.

Garrett could feel Ving's hot gaze burning a hole in his plan. Unflinching, Garrett squared his shoulders and stood eye to eye with his comrade.

"I don't like it." Ving rubbed his palm over his shaved head and he shifted his weight from one foot to the other. "She's my kid sister."

Jenny spun around and glared at him. "I'm *his* kid sister," she countered and pointed at Garrett. "And he never had a problem with us hooking up."

"Yeah, but he's a...he's not a...he doesn't even want..."

As the implication of what he was and what he wasn't hovered over them, Tallulah piped in, "What he is, is a wonderful man, and the most attentive guy a girl could ask for. He's very in tune with my needs and you should see the way he is with kids." They exchanged a long look then she added, "He came to a little boy's rescue on the plane."

She'd noticed that?

She shifted closer. "He'll make an awesome father."

Oddly enough everything from the conviction in her voice to the way she gazed up at him, her eyes honest and sincere, had him wishing it was true. But he knew better.

Jenny clasped her hands and squealed in delight, and once again Garrett couldn't help but admire Tallulah's quick intelligence as she stood up for him. "You're engaged? Already?" She hugged Tallulah. "But then again who am I to talk. When you know it's right, you know it's right." She clasped Tallulah's hand and tugged her from Garrett. "Come on. Let's go grab your luggage and you can tell me all about it."

"Nope," Tallulah said. "Like I said, this week is about you, not me."

As the women walked away, Ving took a threatening step closer. "So help me, if you hurt her."

Garrett patted his old friend on the shoulder. "If I hurt her, you have my permission to kick my ass."

"I'll do more than kick your ass."

"And I wouldn't expect anything less. Now come on. How about I buy the groom a beer? You look like you could use one."

After collecting their luggage, Garrett and Tallulah climbed into the back seat of Ving's SUV. Jenny talked non-stop about the upcoming bridal shower, the dress fittings scheduled for later that day, the bachelorette party, the private get together at the local pub later that night, and how she was so excited about the two of them hooking up. Every time she turned the attention to them, Tallulah turned it right back around again, and lucky for them Jenny was happy to talk about the wedding.

Ving cast him a glance in the rearview mirror and Garrett pulled Tallulah in close to drop a soft kiss onto her cheek. A shudder moved through her body, and no matter what she said about him not being her type, he knew she felt the sexual tension between them every bit as much as he did. He also knew better than to act on it.

"Do Mom and Dad know about this, Tally?" Ving asked.

Tallulah placed her hand on Garrett's thigh, and her heat seeped through his jeans, damn near igniting his blood to boil.

"Not yet," she said. "We thought we'd surprise them."

Jenny beamed at Garrett. "Well, our mom is already at the hotel, and she's going to be thrilled when she hears." Just then Jenny's cell rang and she fished it out of her purse.

As Jenny spoke excitedly into her phone, Garrett leaned in to Tallulah and lowered his voice for her ears only. "It might look odd to our friends if we get two rooms."

"I guess I never thought that far ahead." She nibbled her bottom lip and looked thoughtful for a moment. "Actually I planned to stay with my folks."

"Then I guess I'll stay there with you." When she gave him an odd look, he explained. "People will expect that we'll want to be close to each other."

"You know they'll want us in separate rooms." The hand on his leg relaxed a bit, and as she bit her lip in thought, he suspected she had no idea it was drifting farther up his leg. He clenched his jaw when his blood began flowing hot and heavy, and his muscles tightened, one in particular. Wide eyes blinked up at him and her nose crinkled. "Which is probably for the best, don't you think?"

"Yeah," he agreed, because they both knew this heat between them was explosive, and a locked door and soft bed might be all the spark they needed to ignite the short fuse.

Even though he knew they should sleep apart, he couldn't help but feel an unwise sense of disappointment. She was sweet, sexy, intelligent as hell, and all kinds of wrong for him, but that didn't stop him from wanting to take a small taste. One long, leisurely lick from head to toe.

Shit.

He worked to bank his desires, but his damn cock refused to obey. Maybe he never should have suggested this ruse, because keeping his hands to himself when no one was looking just might be harder than he ever anticipated.

———

The second Ving pulled his SUV into the driveway Tallulah's folks came out to meet her. Tamping down her anxiety, she climbed from the vehicle and rushed up the porch steps to give them a hug. She stole a quick glance around, half expecting to see her ex, Jason Landry, exiting through the swinging screen door behind them.

After they spun her around and did a thorough inspection to ensure the big city hadn't corrupted her, her mother looked past her shoulders to see Garrett coming her way. She tented her fingers. "You must be Jenny's brother. I can see the resemblance."

"That's not all he is," Ving murmured under his breath.

When her mom gave Ving a perplexed look, Tallulah rushed out. "Mom, Dad, this is Garrett Andersen. My fiancé." She turned to Garrett, "This is my mom and dad, Barbara and George Duncan."

Garrett came up the stairs to stand beside Tallulah, his hand outstretched to her father, who looked utterly skeptical, and maybe even a bit perturbed. Not that she could blame him. Garrett wasn't the type of guy they expected her to bring home. Then again, when this was all over, and they faked a breakup, her parents would be happy once again. No harm, no foul. Right? But then, wouldn't she be right back to where she was before this, with her family trying to convince her to move back home because they felt they knew what was best for her? She pushed the thought aside, deciding to cross that bridge when she came to it. Right now she didn't want to spend any more time agonizing over what it would eventually take to convince them otherwise.

Her mom's eyes widened and after shaking Garrett's hand, George glared at the two with obvious suspicion.

"Fiancé?" he asked, his gaze going back and forth between the two. "Now what is this all about, young lady?" He stared at Tallulah but she didn't miss the warmth in his eyes when they met hers.

"Yeah, that's what I want to know," Ving said, and Jenny gave him an elbow to the gut.

"We didn't want to steal Ving and Jenny's thunder," Garrett supplied. "So we kept things on the down low."

"Now that you've spilled the beans, we want to hear all about it," her mother said firmly, and Tallulah couldn't help but squirm under her scrutinizing gaze. "Come on inside. I'll put on the tea." She cast Garrett a harsh look. "I want to learn all about the man who is taking my daughter away." With an efficient clap, her mother began ushering the group inside.

"Jenny and I are going to check on the horses," Ving said, bailing, because he clearly felt a speech coming, every bit as much as Tallulah did.

With Garrett's hand on the small of her back, they

stepped inside the house and she watched the way he glanced around, looking at the baby pictures lining the walls as they walked the long length of the hall.

"You were a cute kid," he whispered. When they reached the kitchen, he pulled her chair out for her. Tallulah caught the way her mother was eyeing them, her probing gaze assessing them both carefully. Garrett sat next to her, and since they'd only really just met, it was odd how comforting it felt just having him there, supporting her as she faced her folks and told them a bold faced lie.

Her mom steeped the tea and cut a loaf of banana bread, then placed it on the table. Her father sat at the head of the table and helped himself to a generous piece. As he chewed he kept his eyes on Tallulah, and she tried not to fidget under his inspection.

"So, you're engaged," her mother said, getting right to the point as she poured sugar into her tea cup and chased it with a spoon.

Tallulah accepted a cup and took a sip while Garrett added milk and sugar to his. "Yes, I thought you'd be thrilled."

She looked pointedly at Tallulah and, never one to beat around the bush, she said, "And here I thought you were coming back home to stay."

Tallulah placed her elbows on the table and began tenting her fingers. Garrett reached out, grabbed her hands in his and pulled them onto his lap.

He gave a reassuring squeeze. "She can't come back now. She's up for the director's position at the day care. She's been working so hard for this and I'm so proud of her."

Her mother took a sip of her tea and stared at Garrett over the rim. "But this is where you belong, Lu. This is where your family is."

Tallulah exhaled slowly, hating the double standards her

parents had for their two kids. But she also knew her folks had been getting on in their years when they adopted her and Ving, and their notions on family roles hadn't changed with the times. Men worked. Women stayed home. Nothing she could do or say would ever change their old-fashioned principals and standards.

"Shouldn't you be thinking about giving up work so you can stay home and have kids?"

"Mom, lots of people work and raise kids," Tallulah said carefully, not wanting to upset anyone. The truth was they only wanted what was best for her, and somehow thought they knew what that was.

"Well this is a much better place to raise a family than that dangerous city you're in."

"I won't let anything happen to her." Garrett put his arm around her in a protective manner, and she met his glance. She caught the possessive way he looked at her, and took a quick breath in a bid to remind herself this wasn't real. "Not that she needs my protection. She's an independent woman and can take care of herself."

Just then her father piped in and turned the conversation to Garrett, grilling him on his work and how he planned to take care of Tallulah now that he'd gotten out of the military.

He told them all about the job he was up for and when he finished Jenny and Ving returned and Tallulah was glad for the interruption.

"We're going to take off," Ving said. "We have some last minute things to take care of before our get together at The Hop Yard tonight."

Tallulah jumped from her chair. "Hang on. I need to get my suitcase."

Her mom set her cup down and narrowed her eyes. "I didn't think you'd be settling in to your old room until after the wedding."

Tallulah's stomach tightened, not liking the sound of this as her glance bobbed between her mother and father. She dropped back down into her chair, and Garrett reached out for her. "What's going on?"

"I gave your bedroom away to Aunt Jo and Uncle Bert. They just drove in for the wedding and are up there resting now."

Tallulah gave a casual shrug and tried to focus on a solution, a difficult task with Garrett's arm around her shoulders. The combination of his heat and enticing scent were melting her brain cells faster than a nuclear explosion.

"That's fine, I'll take Ving's old room," she said, knowing Ving and the rest of the bridal party were all staying at the hotel where the wedding activities were taking place.

"Afraid you can't do that, either." Her father's bushy gray brows knitted together over cloudy blue eyes.

She pulled a worried face and leaned forward in her chair. Garrett's arm fell to the small of her back, his fingers lightly brushing her sensitive skin in a manner that made her wonder how they'd feel moving over another part of her body. A slow burn worked its way through her bloodstream and settled deep between her legs. At least the two would have no problem convincing everyone there was heat between them, a real physical attraction.

"You gave that away too?" she croaked out, struggling to focus her scattered thoughts.

"Your Aunt Betty and Uncle Stan are here too." Apologetic eyes blinked rapidly. "We thought you'd be staying at the hotel with the rest of the bridal party," her mother added.

"I didn't bother to book a room." A nervous feeling settled in the pit of her stomach, because she suspected the hotel would be full by now. If she didn't do something fast she would have to bunk with the hot hunk of a guy sitting next to her, a guy who continually made her rethink her position on one-night stands. "I guess there's always the sofa."

"I can't have one of my bridesmaids sleeping on the sofa. Don't worry, we'll find you a roommate," Jenny said, exchanging a private, knowing look with her, one that said her old-fashioned folks never needed to know that her roommate would be none other than her fiancé.

Her glance went to Garrett, and she noted the intense way he looked at her, his piercing baby blues full of heat as they moved over her face. The air around them charged, and her entire body tightened in a way it had never tightened before as warm shivers of awareness hurried down her spine. She bit the inside of her mouth, acutely aware of the sexy man beside her and all the delicious things they could do together. In an instant she knew sharing a room—a bed— with him would be a very, very bad idea.

Not because she didn't trust him, but because suddenly, she didn't trust herself.

3

As the rest of the bridal party mingled at the private get together at The Hop Yard, the town's oldest pub and hang out, Tallulah took that time to catch up with her best friend Kat—short for Katherine Anne Marie Stiller.

Ignoring the din of the crowd, Kat leaned across the table and shook her head in amazement. Her long chestnut curls spilled down her back, and her emerald-green eyes sparkled with mischief. "I don't know how you did it, Lu. You leave here a sweet and naïve girl only to come back with the hottest guy I've ever set eyes on." Her dreamy glance flickered to Garrett, who was playing a round of pool with Ving and a few other guys, before flittering back to Tallulah. She smacked her lips in delight. "I bet he's done all kinds of delicious things to corrupt you."

"Kat," she admonished, not at all surprised by her friend's boldness. The two might have been best friends since kindergarten, but Kat was the antithesis of Tallulah in every way possible. Not only was her friend a wild child who went after what she wanted, with no regrets in the morning, she spoke her mind, did just about anything on a dare, and never let anyone push her around or tell her what was best for her.

With heat and strength radiating from him, Garrett leaned against the wall, his pool cue balanced in one hand while he took a long pull from his beer bottle. "Holy Hell, talk about testosterone in a T-shirt." Kat's glance panned him once again, then her grin widened naughtily when he pushed off the wall, and bent over the table to take a shot. "Look at that ass." She let loose a long whistle, took a sip of her fruity drink and winked before saying, "He looks great in a pair of jeans but I bet he looks even better out of them."

Tallulah's mind raced, certain her friend was right, but not wanting to spend any more time thinking about Garrett's ass, in or out of jeans, otherwise she might never be able to behave herself behind closed doors tonight.

"If all the guys in Texas look like that, then maybe I'll make that move to Austin sooner rather than later."

Tallulah fiddled with the thick silver band on her finger, and as she thought about the man who put it there—a man she'd soon be sharing a bed with—warm ribbons of heat licked through her. She blinked to clear the erotic visions, wanting to think about something else beside the two of them under the covers together.

She focused on Kat. "You know you're always welcome to stay with me until you find a place of your own, and I'm sure the hospital could use another great physical therapist."

"I wouldn't want to interfere...if you know what I mean."

Tallulah gave a feeble smile, guilt eating at her for not telling her best friend the truth.

"So tell me," Kat began, her eyes glinting. "Does he have a...you know?"

Certain this was a conversation she didn't want to be having in public, or private, or anywhere for that matter,

Tallulah took a huge sip of her daiquiri and said, "No, I don't know."

"Come on, Lu." Kat exhaled an exaggerated breath. "Help a friend out. I've been on such a dry spell lately that the least you can do is tell me all about your sex life so I can live vicariously through you."

"Why have you been on a dry spell?"

Kat slouched in her seat. "The guys around here are so damn dull. Christ, they couldn't find a woman's g-spot even with the aid of GPS. Then again," she added, looking like the cat about to swallow the canary, "now that Ving's army pals are all here for the wedding things are definitely starting to look *up*." She stopped and narrowed her eyes. "Hey, stop trying to change the subject. We're talking about you and your sex life here, not mine."

Tallulah lifted her chin. "I don't kiss and tell."

Kat gave a cheeky grin. "It's not his kissing I'm asking about. What I want to know about lies a little farther south." Kat finished off her drink, slid it across the table and said, "But if you really need to me spell it out for you, I'm wondering if he has a big cock and just how good he is at using it. Does he use it like a jackhammer and make you come hard?"

Tallulah choked on an ice cube, shock widening her eyes. "Ah, I think we should talk about something else."

"Fine, but I'll get the truth out of you yet. I always do." Kat leaned back in her chair, gestured for the waitress to bring two more drinks, then compressed her lips in worry. In a serious voice she asked, "Does Jason know?"

Tallulah's gut clenched. "I'm sure he does by now. When we left Mom's she was already reaching for the phone."

"News travel faster than brush fire around these parts. How do you think he's going to react?"

"We were never in love, Kat, and he just wanted a

dutiful wife on his arm when dealing with grieving families. To him I was a safety net in case he didn't meet anyone else. To his family I was the nice girl they deemed suitable for the position of wife and assistant to the funeral director."

Kat nodded in total agreement. "You're right, but now that Jason has taken over his father's business I can't blame you for not wanting to be an undertaker's wife. It's creepy." She shivered, and pulled a sour face that conveyed her distaste. Then again, Kat never was a fan of Jason's. She said there was another side to him, and one day it would end up coming out.

After the waitress delivered two more drinks, Kat took a huge sip and shook her head. "I still can't believe you didn't tell me you were engaged, or that you were even dating such an Adonis."

Tallulah's stomach turned at the genuine sadness on her friend's face, and honestly she couldn't blame Kat for being upset. They'd shared everything over the years, and keeping secrets from her best friend—especially something as big as this one—was out of character for Tallulah.

Once again guilt settled heavy in her gut and she reached out and closed her hand over Kat's, needing in the most desperate ways to tell her friend the truth. Kat had her back, and would keep her secret. She always had before and there was a good chance she might need her friend to run interference at some point. Besides, if she didn't tell someone soon, she feared she'd burst at the seams, and all the lies would come spilling out at once.

"I need to tell you something."

Sulking, and feigning disinterest, Kat waved a dismissive hand. "Unless it's all the dirty details of your sex life I don't want to hear it."

"Oh, believe me, you're going to want to hear this."

Kat sat up straighter, her interest clearly piqued. "Oh yeah? Do tell then."

Tallulah shifted her chair closer, and looked around to make sure they couldn't be overheard. When she spotted Garrett watching her, a hungry gleam in those perceptive blue eyes, ribbons of heat reverberated through her blood. She shivered, almost violently, then exhaled slowly as she turned her focus back to her friend.

"Wow," Kat said after witnessing the exchange. She fanned her face and pushed her chair back on two legs. "I can feel the heat between you two from here."

"We're not engaged," Tallulah confessed.

Kat's head came back with a start, the front legs of her chair slamming down on the old plank floor. "What are you talking about, Lu?"

Tallulah lowered her voice even more. "It's a ruse. He's not my fiancé. Not really."

"Whoa!" Kat said. "What the hell is going on?"

She told Kat the whole story, relaying every detail from how they met on the plane to how Garrett thought they could both help each other out by pretending they were engaged. She even went so far as to tell Kat how they touched, and shared a kiss, in an effort to better acquaint themselves and make it look real.

After taking a moment to absorb everything, Kat said, "I don't know why you don't just tell Jason you moved on and the pact was a stupid idea."

"I just don't want to get into it with him, or battle with my folks." Her hand closed over her stomach. "Besides, I actually considered going through with it for a while there."

Kat gave her hand a reassuring squeeze, concern moving into her eyes. "Don't worry, Lu. You'll get your baby. One way or another you'll get your baby. You'll see."

Even though she wasn't so sure herself, Tallulah loved her

friend's support, loved that Kat was in her corner no matter what. Tallulah nodded and returned the comforting squeeze. "Just keep this between us, okay?"

"You know your secret is safe with me." Kat lowered her voice to match Tallulah's and asked, "So what's in it for Garrett? Does he get to exercise his fiancé rights?" She arched a curious yet hopeful brow. "Please tell me that's how you'll be helping him out."

"No, nothing like that. Just a little tit for tat."

"Oooh, I like the sounds of that even better."

Tallulah rolled her eyes. "Get your mind out of the gutter. What I mean is I'll be pretending to be his fiancée back home to help him land a job."

Kat frowned. "Well that's boring."

"It's not boring...it just is. Besides," she added, "he's not my type."

Kat threw her head back and gave a big loud belly laugh, seeing right through her fib. But, Kat knew her better than anyone so it shouldn't have surprised Tallulah. "Oh yeah right. Who are you trying to kid? He's every woman's type. Even my eighty-year-old grandma would be standing in line to go a few rounds with him."

Tallulah couldn't help but smile, small butterflies taking flight in her stomach as she stole another glance at her betrothed. She couldn't deny that he was the sexiest guy in the room, his mere presence garnering quite a bit of attention from the other members of the bridal party.

"Okay, fine. You're right," she conceded. "I'm attracted to him but we're nothing alike and he's not into long-term relationships, which means its hands off behind closed doors."

Kat wagged her finger back and forth between the two of them. "Hey, if you don't think opposites attract, just look at us. And besides, who said anything about having a relationship?"

Tallulah folded her hands on the countertop. "You know me better than that, Kat. I don't do one-night stands."

"Maybe not, but you've just been given a free ticket, girlfriend. He's your fiancé, pretend or not, and if I were you I'd be enjoying the benefits that came with that. As long as you have no expectations coming *out*, then you should be seriously letting him *in*, if you know what I mean."

Oh, she knew what she meant. They both turned their attention to their frosty drinks, and silence hovered as they became lost in their own thoughts.

After a long moment, Kat broke the quiet, leaned in to her and asked, "So what do you think? Are you going to seduce him?"

Tallulah's stomach lurched. She'd dated in Austin, of course. Even had a couple long-term relationships, but she'd never straight up and seduced a guy before. "I'm not even sure I'd know how."

"Then it's a good thing you got me," Kat said, giving her a smug look.

"Oh?"

"Yeah, here's what you do. Tonight when you both go back to your room, slip into something short and slinky and bend over a lot."

Tallulah laughed, but when she saw the calculating look on her friend's face, it quickly dissolved. "Wait! You're serious aren't you?"

"If you want to seduce this guy, then you should listen to me. I know what I'm talking about."

Tallulah planted her elbows on the table and rested her chin in her palms. "I'd hate to be the guy who tried to tame you, Kat. He's in for one hell of a ride."

"Tame me? Hell, girlfriend, no guy is ever going to break my will." She gave a playful wink. "Of course I might let him bend it a little. Bending is always fun."

They shared a laugh, then Tallulah caught Garrett's glance once again. When those deep eyes were looking directly at her, she forgot every serious thought, forgot why keeping her distance was a good idea.

Then again, if she knew what she was getting herself into...

"Maybe I should just share a room with you."

Kat eyed Matt James, Ving's best man, as he cut across the floor. "Sure, if you don't mind joining a party of two." Then she said, "Come on, Tallulah, if you don't share his room, you're going to blow your cover. And if I were you, there are other things I'd be thinking about blowing."

Tallulah groaned. "It won't work, Kat. I don't have anything short or slinky."

"No problem. Tell him you forgot your nightgown and ask to borrow one of his T-shirts. Guys dig that kind of shit."

Tallulah took a moment to visualize herself in his shirt, his warm scent engulfing her as the rough material brushed over her sensitive flesh. Her skin tightened and her nipples hardened almost painfully as she pictured herself parading around in something so skimpy, bending over to pick up some imaginary object and seducing him out of his pants. God, it was just so indecent. So naughty.

So not her.

But oh how she wanted it to be. Honest to God, she might be inexperienced in the art of seduction, but when it came right down to it she was damn tired of vanilla sex. The guys she'd been with—the marrying kind—cared little about her needs and left her wanting so much more. But Garrett... she'd just bet he'd never walk away leaving a woman unsatisfied. No, he might not be the marrying kind—the kind her mother expected her to bring home—but he most definitely was the kind to give her earth-shattering sex that would totally rock the hell right out of her world.

She'd be crazy to turn her back on the opportunity,

wouldn't she? After all, they were both consenting adults, and, for all intents and purposes, they were engaged.

Just then Garrett leaned over the table, that sexy ass of his taunting her libido and urging her to go for it. While her body trembled, aching to know what it would be like to be touched by his hands, his mouth...his tongue, there was a part of her brain that warned her to walk—no, run—the other away. But then again there was another small, reckless part of her, one that demanded she shed her inhibitions and step out of character for just one night. Could she really do that? She felt a quick flash of panic, then drew a breath to calm herself.

Tallulah shook her head. "This is a really, really bad idea."

"Yes it is," Kat agreed with a sassy grin. "But aren't those the best kind?"

———

"You want to get your mind off my damn sister and back on to the game," Ving scowled, and jabbed his elbow into Garrett's stomach with much more force than necessary.

Turning his attention to the table as the gut punch jostled him back to the present, Garrett scanned the balls, placed his beer bottle on the edge, then bent over to take the winning shot. "Double or nothing?" he asked as the eight ball slid into the corner pocket.

Ving tossed a few bills on the table. "I'm out," he announced when Jenny came sidling up to him.

She gave him a wink. "Hey, fly boy, you want to call it a night?"

Ving offered Garrett his back and turned his full attention to Jenny. Warmth sounded in his voice when he answered with, "Hell yeah."

Ving slipped his arm around Jenny's shoulders, but before they left, she turned back to Garrett, "Don't forget about the bridal luncheon tomorrow. Twelve sharp in the hotel restaurant.”

“Or the bachelor party tomorrow night,” Ving added, a wry grin tugging the corners of his mouth up as he cast Garrett a quick glance. “Nine sharp.” He pointed downward. “Right here.”

Jenny placed her hand on Ving’s shoulder, her big diamond ring glistening in the overhead lights. “Now that Garrett is spoken for, at least I don’t have to worry about him corrupting you tomorrow night.”

Speaking of corrupting…

Garrett angled his head in time to see Tallulah watching him, her friend Kat grinning mischievously as she whispered something in Tallulah’s ear. After a quick trip to their shared hotel room earlier that evening to drop off their luggage, Tallulah had changed into a country girl dress fit for any sweet and sensitive daycare teacher. Everything about her screamed inexperience, and while that dress would make any church-going parent proud, it turned Garrett inside out, his mind conjuring up naughty images. Images like peeling it from her lush body, laying her out on the king-size bed they were forced to share, and showing her just how good he could make it for her. His cock thickened, and a low growl crawled out of his throat.

Jesus, she really was sweet and innocent, and so damn easy to like, which gave credence to his logic to keep his distance. He associated with “one night” kind of women for a reason. They never asked him for anything more than a good, hard fuck. At least between the sheets he’d never let anyone down.

Just then Brad Crosby, Garrett’s childhood best friend and fellow comrade came up to the table and grabbed the rack. Garrett pulled the balls from the pockets and rolled them down the table.

“So, Tallulah, huh?” Brad asked, his perceptive eyes

gauging Garrett's reactions as he gathered the balls and arranged them in the rack.

"Yeah, that's right."

Brad's gaze catalogued the room before settling on Tallulah, and oddly enough, Garrett didn't like the way his friend looked at her, locking her in his cross hairs like a predator marking its prey. "I never thought I'd see the day a woman ball and chained you, pal."

Ignoring him, Garrett tossed a coin, and called heads to see who'd go first.

Brad widened his stance, his shrewd glance assessing Garrett. "It's almost hard to believe."

"Well, believe it," Garrett said, and chalked his cue before breaking.

As the balls scattered, Brad looked at Tallulah again and gave a low wolf whistle. "If she wasn't attached—"

"Well she is, so back the fuck off." Garrett's reaction was strong, stronger than it should have been considering they were merely pretending to be engaged, but hell, at least it would go a long way in convincing his friend this scam was real.

Brad held his hands up palms out in a truce. "Whoa, easy, Garrett."

"Just back off, okay?"

"Come on. You know I'd never hone in on your territory."

It was true. Garrett knew that that. The two went way back, and cared a hell of a lot about each other. Honestly, he loved the guy, he really did. Brad wasn't just his best friend, he was his brother—blood or not—and Garrett would die for him any day. But when it came to women Brad was even more fucked up than Garrett, which meant he was the last guy a nice girl like Tallulah needed to be around.

Brad gave a shake of his head. "Strange how this is the first I've heard about it."

"Nothing strange about it. We were just keeping things low key."

"Hmm."

"What?"

"So I take it I'm going to be your best man."

He gave a noncommittal shrug. "Yeah, sure."

A long pause and then suspicious eyes moved to the white band where his pinky ring used to be. "She must be pretty special if you gave her your dad's ring."

A lump gathered in Garrett's throat at the mention of the ring. Only Brad could know how much he treasured the ring his father had willed to him—a ring his old man had received for exceptional bravery on his job—because Brad was the one who'd found Garrett the night after the funeral, drunk as a goddamn skunk, and babbling about how much of a fuckup he was.

He forced himself not to think about the engraving on the inside band. Shit, everyone wrote nice things on the heirlooms they left to their children, right? He knew his father wasn't proud of him. Never had been. And why would he be? Unlike his sister, Garrett was a lousy student, preferring hands-on and relying on instincts over books, which meant he never got the grades. When it came to sports, Garrett excelled at baseball, but a fight over a bad call got him kicked out of the dugout the day the scouts came to town.

Then, if that wasn't enough, not only did he and his dad butt heads on just about everything, Garrett rebelled when his father wanted him to follow in his footsteps. Even though Garrett wanted to join the police force, he knew he would only end up disappointing the man who was larger than life, a man who was undaunted by anyone or anything. Garrett joined the army instead, hoping on some level he could save the world and earn his father's approval, and maybe even his own. Except he couldn't save anyone, and could barely take care of himself. The scar on his face was proof of that.

Even after his father had died of heart disease Garrett continued to let the family down, continued to show the old man there was no reason to be proud of his only son. If Garrett had of been a stand-up guy, he would have refused his last tour and stayed home to step into his father's role and help the family, but instead he jumped at the chance to flee, running away when Jenny—who was going through a rebellious stage—and his mom needed him the most.

Brad took a shot and the sound of the balls clanging pulled him back. "So about that ring..." he began.

"Yeah, she's special, Brad. Very special. Let's just leave it at that."

"Then why don't you tell me—"

With his mood souring he said, "Why don't you just drop it?"

Brad stepped closer, until he was straight up in Garrett's face. Not one bit afraid of confrontation, he said, "Not until you cut the shit and tell me what's really going on."

Fuck.

Garrett knew better than to think Brad would let it go. The guy was a hard-assed son of a bitch who had an opinion on everything. Although when it really came right down to it, Garrett knew his childhood friend only had his best interests at heart. But Christ, sometimes he wished his comrade couldn't read him so well, and would keep his nose out of Garrett's business. Then again, if the roles were reversed Garrett wouldn't drop it either, and would beat the living crap out of his friend until he got the truth.

"Okay," Garrett said, "But this stays between us."

A few minutes later, after Garrett explained the scam, Brad folded his arms and asked, "Are you sure you know what you're doing?"

"Yeah, I do."

Brad turned his attention to Tallulah and clicked his tongue. "A sweet thing like Tallulah could easily take you down a path you have no intentions of going, and no doubt get you in to all kinds of trouble, don't you think?"

"Not a chance. I've got it all under control."

Brad gave an easy shrug. "Okay, if you say so. But if I were you, I'd get on over there and lay stake to your claim. Unless you're up for a brawl." Brad eyed the crowd and in a show of alliance he pushed his sleeves up. "It's been a while."

Garrett scanned the room and that's when he noticed the way the single guys, and a few of the married ones, were eyeing Tallulah. "Shit," he murmured and fisted his hands, fighting down an unwise pang of jealousy. Not about to start a brawl at his sister's party, he said, "I'll catch you later," and walked to the bar. After stealing a glance at Tallulah's drink, he ordered a beer for himself and another daiquiri for her.

With a crook of his finger, he gestured for her to come close. Without pause, she excused herself from the group of guys who had gathered at her table and crossed the room. When she reached him, he widened his legs and pulled her in between. He slid one hand around her back, and noted the way her slim body fit between his thighs so nicely. He filled his lungs with her scent, and tried not to think about how much he'd like to pay homage to the hard nipples pressing insistently against his chest.

"So what do you think, Peaches?" he asked, his gaze going to her mouth. "Do we have everyone convinced?"

She gave an edgy laugh then looked over her shoulder. "I hope so."

He narrowed his eyes and caught her friend's glance. "You told Kat, didn't you?"

"I can't keep anything from her." She frowned, looked down and added, "Like you said, I'm an easy read."

Something inside him softened when he glimpsed self-reprimand in her eyes. His heart pinched, and forgetting about the crowd watching, he cupped her chin and lifted it until her eyes met his. He gave her a smile and lowered his voice. "It's not a bad thing, Tallulah. Believe me it's not a bad thing."

She shrugged. "It is when you're trying to fool everyone. Even you knew that I told Kat." She angled her head, her eyes assessing him as her glance panned his face. "I can't keep anything from you, can I?"

"Afraid not."

She nodded in acceptance. "Well, at least we don't have to worry about Kat."

"She won't let the *cat* out of the bag?" he teased in an attempt to lighten her mood.

"Wow, I never heard that one before." She laughed and rolled her eyes before adding, "Our secret is safe with her, and she gave me lots of advice."

"Advice?" he asked.

Her eyes widened like she'd said too much. "Nothing. It's nothing," she answered, blinking rapidly, and while he knew there was something she wasn't telling him, with everyone still watching he was well aware that it was time for showing, not telling, so he didn't press.

Instead, he cupped the back of her head and drew her mouth to his for a mind-numbing kiss. When his tongue slipped inside to taste her, he briefly wondered if the kiss had more to do with him needing a nibble than convincing the crowd they were lovers.

Either way, he pulled her impossibly closer, and deepened the kiss for a more thorough taste. Her breasts felt swollen, hot against his chest, and he noticed the movement of her hips. It was slight, but a sexy, needy movement nonetheless. Heat settled deep in his groin, and everything inside him urged him to answer the demands of his body, to take her back to their room and spend the rest of the night discovering all her little secrets—the ones they hadn't discussed on the plane.

Someone slapped him on the shoulder. "Get a room, you two."

Garrett pulled back, Brad's words knocking some common sense back into him before he did something he could only regret later.

He took a deep breath to get himself together. Once he could think at half capacity, he gestured with a nod toward the door. "Maybe we should get out of here. I don't know about you but it's been a long day and I'm ready to hit the sack." He gave her an intimate whack on the ass for show, then climbed to his feet. Her groin bumped his as he stood, and he tried not to think about the tremor that moved through his body.

Her palm went to his chest and she made a move to pull back, but he anchored her to him, partly to keep up the charade and partly because he liked the feel of her soft body next to his. He settled his hands on her waist, and when she trembled, reacting to his touch, his desire mounted tenfold.

Brad plunked himself down on the stool next to him. "Okay, Garrett, we get it. Now get the fuck out of here before I take her from you and show her what a real man can do."

Tallulah gave Garrett a curious glance and he confessed, "Best friend. I spilled too." He narrowed his eyes in warning. "And stay away from him. He's trouble." With that Garrett grabbed Tallulah's hand and headed for the door. They hopped into a cab and a few minutes later they found themselves back at the hotel.

He stole a glance at Tallulah as they stepped onto the waiting elevator and saw the way she worried her bottom lip.

Once they reached their room, he inserted the key card, pushed open the door and guided her in.

"Show's over," he said in a bid to convince Tallulah, as well as himself, that they were safely behind closed doors and could end the charade. That's when he noticed he still had her hand in his.

He quickly let it go and she glanced around the room, her gaze flittering over the furnishing before settling on the big, king-size bed.

As much as he'd like to toss her on that comfy looking bed and have his wicked way with her, he took note of her apprehension, tore off his T-shirt and dropped it onto the bed. "I'll take the floor."

Still standing at the door, looking like a scared church mouse ready to run she said, "You don't have to do that."

Garrett turned to her and froze. Her gaze slid over his naked torso. Shit, if she kept looking at him like that and... oh, God, licking her lips...he'd never be able to keep his hands off her.

"I don't mind," he managed between gritted teeth.

"But it's hard."

Oh, it was hard all right.

"I'm used to hard." Shit, as soon as the words left his mouth he realized how suggestive they sounded. Backtracking he said, "I mean, the ground has been my bed for years, so don't worry about it."

"I'm not worried about it."

"Then what are you worried about?"

"It's just that...well...I...uh...I forget my nightgown. You wouldn't happen to have a spare T-shirt I could borrow, would you?" He reached into his suitcase but stilled when she crossed the room to grab the one he was just wearing. "This one will do."

4

S weet Mother of God and all that was holy!

He'd never taken Tallulah as the clumsy sort—a rambler when nervous, yes, but never clumsy—which meant one thing, and one thing only. She was bending over and driving him mad on purpose.

He raked his fingers through his hair and tried not to look. But who was he kidding. Although he couldn't quite classify what he was doing as looking. No, it was more like gawking. Wide-eyed and immobile, he stood there staring at her like some sort of voyeur who got his rocks off from spying on others.

The shirt he'd given her to wear climbed up the back of her legs, and he nearly sobbed when it almost exposed the soft curve of her ass. Jesus H. Christ, either she was trying to drive him insane, or she was hell bent on getting him into that bed with her. He clenched his jaw hard enough to grind bone, and when she dropped her novel for the umpteenth time, he stepped in to help her.

"Here, let me get that."

He picked the book up and turned it over in his hands.

When he caught a glimpse of the cover, and noticed it was that very popular book that had been all over the news for months, he cast her a curious glance, never expecting a sweet thing like her to be reading such naughty material. His mind instantly flashed to the image of her bound to the headboard, completely at his mercy, his to do with as he pleased, and his heart damn near palpitated right out of his chest.

"Thanks," she murmured, their hands brushing as she took it from him. Shockwaves rocketed through his body, and he fought the natural inclination to give in to temptation and pin her against the wall where he could kiss a path down her body, going lower and lower until he reached the spot that his tongue craved the most.

Christ, talk about a serious reversal of roles here. This sweet and innocent girl was all kinds of contradictions, and he was intelligent enough to know that she was acting out of character, and she'd calculated this seduction, right down to borrowing his clothes. Tallulah Duncan was trying to coax him into her bed. *Him*. A guy who never ran away from a good fuck. Until now.

But she was different. Everything about her screamed danger. Which meant that no way, no how was he going to give in to temptation. Ever.

She stepped away, her sweet ass dragging his focus. "You don't mind if I read for awhile do you?" she asked and perched herself on the edge of the mattress, his T-shirt riding high on her sexy thighs.

She looked so fucking sexy sitting there in his clothes, the plunging neckline on his too-big T-shirt affording him a view of her cleavage, with her nipples pressing against the thin material that it was all he could do to keep his cock in his pants.

He shifted, uncomfortable, and angled his body to hide

the evidence of his raging hard on. "No, go ahead. I need a shower anyway."

Determined to keep his shit together, Garrett made his way to the bathroom. He shut and bolted the door behind him, locking her out and him in before he did something that he'd kick his own ass for in the morning. He turned on the cold water and once it was freezing he climbed inside. A yelp crawled out of his throat as the frigid needle-like spray cooled his hot body.

He stayed under the nozzle for a good long time, and hoped that when he was done, Tallulah had finished reading that sex book of hers and fallen into a deep sleep. After turning off the tap, he towel dried, and pulled on his boxers. He grabbed his clothes from the floor and cautiously inched the door open to peek out. When he caught sight of Tallulah bent over the bed, her curvaceous ass barely covered by his T-shirt as she fluffed her pillow, he gave a low, slow groan.

The sound gained her attention. She tossed him a glance over her shoulder, her long hair spilling over her back in provocative ways that nearly rendered him senseless.

"Everything okay?" she asked.

"Fine," he managed to spit out past the lump in his throat as he crossed the room. He dropped his clothes onto the chair beside the bed, grabbed a pillow and tossed it onto the floor.

She blinked at him and patted the mattress. Long lashes flashed over come-hither eyes. "It really is a big bed, and it would be foolish of me to let you to take the floor when that whole side is empty." There was something very suggestive in her eyes when she lowered her voice and added, "Besides, sleeping together is what engaged couples do, isn't it?"

Garrett looked at the soft bed, and the sexy woman sitting cross-legged on the other end of the mattress, his T-shirt pulled between her legs. Goddammit he knew he'd never be able to keep his hands to himself if he crawled in there with her. Even from across the room, the sweet smell of her skin drove him bat-shit crazy.

"I'll take the floor."

She pursed her lips and after a long thoughtful moment countered with, "I've been thinking. This is your room, so by rights I should be the one sleeping on the floor."

"You're not sleeping on the floor."

"No, it's only fair." She tossed her pillow down and climbed from the soft mattress, determination etched on her pretty face.

"Look," he began, running anxious hands through his hair as she stood there staring at him, looking like a sex-kitten that he'd do just about anything to hear purr. "I'm not going to take the bed and let you sleep on the floor. Not when we have a king-size mattress that could easily sleep five."

A smug look came over her face. "Exactly," she said, and he somehow felt that he'd just been duped. She blinked up at him with bright-eyed innocence as she bent over to pick up her pillow. Jesus Christ, she really needed to stop all that fucking bending!

"And don't worry. I'll try to refrain from touching you," she said, tossing his teasing words back at him.

She flicked the lamp off and once she was under the covers, Garrett climbed into his side, keeping his back to her and his face toward the window. Clinging to the edge, he pulled the covers over his chest and concentrated on getting his breathing—and his hard-on—under control.

Since he hadn't bothered to shut the curtains, moonlight poured over the bed, and he struggled to focus on something other than the woman beside him. He thought about work, his tours overseas, walking Jenny down the aisle.

Tallulah.

Goddammit. He lifted his head and punched his pillow,

unable to get comfortable. Even with the slant of light, the room seemed to close in on him, the air growing heavier, more suffocating, by the minute. Silence hung for a long time, and the bed felt warm, hot even, making the tension between them that much more palpable.

She made a restless noise and shifted beside him, breaking the quiet. Garrett squeezed his eyes shut, staying still. Perfectly still.

"Garrett."

Don't answer. Don't do it. Pretend you're asleep.

"Yeah."

Dammit.

Her voice was low, barely audible when she said, "We have the luncheon tomorrow and my entire family is going to be there."

The worry in her voice did him in. With a sigh, he rolled onto his back. Her body heat reached out to him and fucked with his libido in ways he'd never before known. He worked to leash his control but his cock was so hard, craving the feel of her heat wrapped around it. Sweat beaded on his brow and upper lip. "And?"

"I'm a little worried."

"What about?"

"What if we can't pull this off?"

He shifted to his side to face her, and the second their eyes met, sparks leapt between them and nearly set the room ablaze. Her long loose curls tumbled in silken waves over the pillowcase, the erotic image straight out of his fantasy. Blood left his brain in a whoosh and headed south until his cock was at full attention, standing tall and erect like any good soldier ready to dive into battle head first. *Head first... Ah, Jesus.* He sucked in a breath but couldn't seem to fill his oxygen starved lungs.

"It will be fine."

"What if I blow it? I mean I blew it with Kat tonight."

"Don't worry about it. I told Brad too."

"I don't know, Garrett." She exhaled an exaggerated breath. "We all know I'm an easy read, and what if...?"

Her voice fell off and common sense urged him to roll back over and let it go, to put an end to this conversation before it got him into a shit load of trouble. But with raw hunger overshadowing sensibility, he probed, "What are you worried about?"

"What if you touch me somewhere I'm not expecting it and I...flinch."

His heart thundered in his chest, his body begging him to put her worries to rest by pulling her beneath him and touching her all over, with his hands, his mouth, his tongue. But he wasn't going to. No, he understood she wasn't a girl who took sex lightly—he'd seen it in her eyes, read it in her every gesture—and he wasn't sure what kind of game she was playing, but he'd be damned if he was going to play it with her.

He cleared his throat. "Don't worry. You won't."

"How can you be so sure? If I couldn't fool Kat, how will I ever be able to convince my entire family we're a real couple? I mean, just say you touch me and I flinch, they'll know in an instant something isn't right."

"I touched you tonight and you didn't flinch."

"Yeah, that's true." Her voice dropped to a soft whisper when she added, "But you didn't touch me here."

He heard the sheets rustle and her arms moved beneath them. Unable to help himself, he visualized her putting her hands on her body, her breasts, between her legs. His cock swelled. Christ, he should have released the pressure in the shower. She made a sexy noise and the mattress dipped near him as she shimmied closer.

With her body only inches from his, his rock hard cock

screamed at him to do something, like climb over her body and impale her until he gave them what they both wanted. He groaned in frustration, using every ounce of strength he possessed to keep his hands to himself. Okay, he needed to get the fuck out of her bed and he needed to do it now.

Walk away, Garrett, just walk away.

"Where didn't I touch you?"

Ah, fuck.

She rolled onto her back as his fingers crept across the mattress. When he reached her stomach, he brushed her flesh lightly, drawing small circles over her abdomen with his thumb. He listened to her breathing change, become more erratic, and he fought valiantly to keep his shit together.

Her hand closed over his. "Here," she said, as she guided his palm to her breasts. "You didn't touch me here," she purred, her sultry invitation smashing his resolve in seconds flat.

As soon as he felt her soft breast encased in his large palm, he gulped air and despite lecturing himself earlier, every fiber of his being was ready to give in to temptation. She was so needy, so hot for him that all he could think about was giving her a good long fuck until she trembled in his arms, until they both walked away satisfied.

"What are you doing, Tallulah?" he asked, understanding they both knew he'd never touch her breasts in public, and this game she was playing had nothing to do with the charade.

"I just want to make sure we don't blow this," she answered, the want—no, the need—he heard in her voice snapping his last vestige of control.

With rational thought obliterated, his brain shut down, and that's when primal instincts took over.

"And you think if I touch you here now," he asked, lightly

caressing the soft pad of his thumb over her nipples until they formed tight peaks, "that it will help?"

She gave a broken gasp and pressed against him, her hot breath tickling the fine hair on his neck and fragmenting his thoughts. "I think it's a good start."

He stroked the underside of her breast and her eyes glimmered with dark sensuality. Struggling to think, to form a rational sentence he asked, "Where else do you think I should touch you?"

In a bold move that both surprised and excited him, she grabbed his hand and pushed it downward.

Following her direction, he slid his hand lower until he reached her bellybutton. Stroking her stomach through his cotton T-shirt, he asked, "Here? You think it will help if I touch you here?"

"I don't think it can hurt," she murmured, her body burning up beneath his hands. He splayed his fingers over her stomach and held her down while he shifted closer, until his cock pressed insistently against her leg.

Her small gasp prompted him into action and even though some small coherent part of his brain told him this was a bad idea, his brain was no longer calling the shots. He slipped his hand under her shirt, and when he caught the tang of her arousal, felt the heat of her flesh, his mouth watered for a taste.

The softness of her skin, the sweet perfumed scent of her firm body, engulfed him as he trailed his fingers over her sides, shaping her contours as he dipped lower and lower. He skimmed her pubis and briefly closed his eyes against the flood of heat.

"What about here, Peaches?" he whispered with effort. "Do you think I should touch you here?"

In a voice full of want, she murmured, "I think it would be a good idea. You know, for the ruse."

Without preamble, he threw back the sheet and went up on his knees, crawling between her legs. In the moonlight, her eyes dimmed with desire, making her look so damn sexy. He gripped her thighs and spread them. With the tips of his finger, he skimmed her silken flesh, allowing her seductive scent to singe his nerve endings. Too far gone to stop himself now, he ran his hand higher and higher until he came perilously close to her sweet spot.

Knowing he needed to slow down before he ravaged her caveman style, he drew a centering breath. "Are you sure, Tallulah?" he asked and when she nodded, he ran his fingers under the skimp of material along her hips, until he reached the lace band on her pubis. He gripped the material, shifted to the side, and slid her panties down her legs, prolonging the seduction in an effort to make her as crazy as she was making him.

He slipped them off and as he climbed back between her legs, he dangled the panties around his index finger. "Mmmm, pink. My favorite color."

Taking them to a whole new level of intimacy, he ran his finger along the soft seam covering the spot his mouth craved the most, inching her pussy lips open until her pretty pink sex was exposed. He went back on his heels and perused her body.

"Jesus, Tallulah, you have the prettiest pussy I've ever seen." His mouth went dry as he stared long and hard, taking his sweet time to commit every inch of her to memory.

Taking pleasure in the sensual sight before him, his fingers widened her sex even more. When their glances met and locked, he asked, "What about here, Peaches? Should I touch you here?"

The first furtive brush over her clit had her hips coming off the bed. "Yes," she cried out, arousal edging her voice as her hands tangled around his neck. "Definitely there."

Christ, he loved how she responded to him. So eager. So open. So damn pliable in his arms.

His body tightened, and no longer able to ignore his craving, he lightly brushed her wet pussy, stroking all the way from the bottom to the top as he climbed up her body, pulling the T-shirt up to free her beautiful breasts. Pinning her beneath him, his lips crashed down on hers. Her mouth opened and he kissed her long and deep. His tongue sweeping inside to mate with hers before he buried his face in the soft crook of her neck.

He ran his lips over her sensitive flesh, then grabbed her hands to pin them above her head, the way he'd fantasized when he caught her reading that damn book. Once he had her captive beneath him, he turned his attention to her perfect breasts, her pale pink nipples to be specific. With little finesse and much greed, he drew one hard bud into his mouth, relishing the feel and texture as he laved her with the tip of his tongue. He circled her velvety areola, then sucked and nibbled until she began writhing like a wanton woman.

"Garrett," she cried out, her body moving, craving so much more.

"Yeah?" he asked. "What is it? Do you think I should put my mouth somewhere else?"

"Yes, please," she answered, the hunger in her voice raising his passion to new heights.

He freed one of her hands. "Show me where," he said, needing in the most desperate ways for her to not only take—but demand—what she wanted.

Without speaking she pushed on his shoulder until his mouth was inches from her pussy.

"That's a girl," he said, and since he craved to taste the sweetness between her legs, she didn't have to ask him twice. He better positioned himself, stopping to tease her belly-button before reaching the hot apex of her legs.

He caught a glimpse of her pussy glistening in the moonlight, her lips damp from passion. His cock pulsed in response. "Baby, you are so fucking hot and wet that you've got me right there."

"Please, Garrett," she begged and with that he pressed his mouth to her sex.

He licked deep, tasting every inch of her, then glanced heavenward. His nostrils flared and he shook his head in sheer agony. Peaches...oh sweet fuck, she tasted just like peaches. She was going to be the death of him yet.

Turning his attention back to the woman beneath him, he lightly brushed her clit before inserting a finger, and when he felt her close around him, her walls so tight, he pinched his eyes shut and worked to hang on. His cock ached, throbbing to be inside her as he plunged his finger deeper, slowly building her orgasm as he brushed her g-spot.

He thumbed her clit, using slow torturous circles. Tallulah moaned without censor as her body tightened under his erotic assault, letting him know she was close, so close.

"That's it, sweetheart," he encouraged, loving the way she came apart for him.

She gripped his head and arched into him, her sexy moves conveying without words what she needed, how much she liked what he was doing to her.

His body vibrated as her pleasure resonated through him and while he never left a woman unsatisfied, giving this sweet thing everything she needed suddenly became more important than breathing. With her pleasures paramount, he increased the pressure on her g-spot, and tapped her clit, the duel assault eliciting a violent shudder from her.

Jesus...

He could feel the tension escalating inside her, and her body began quaking, trembling with the hot, hard approach of an orgasm.

Giving her no reprieve as he took her to the precipice, he made a slow pass with his tongue, eager to rock her world. She began panting, moisture breaking out on her skin. Her pussy clenched around his finger, and the urgency, the desperation in her eyes when they met his, did strange things to his gut.

He pushed another finger inside her, and the fit was so deliciously tight he questioned how he'd ever get his cock in her. She threw her head back and cried, her body responding with a hot flow of release. She shuddered beneath his ministrations, her hot cream dripping over his hand as she came undone. Desperate for another taste, he leaned forward and licked her, burying his mouth between her legs and drinking her in until her body stopped trembling.

After a long time he sat back on his heels to look at her. He lightly petted her sex, keeping her warm and ready until he could fill her with his cock. When he saw how open she was for him, her body spread and welcoming as her eyes moved over him with desire, he found himself yearning for things he knew better than to long for.

Christ, she was simply amazing, not at all worried about how she sounded or looked while he brought her to orgasm with his mouth and hands. Instead she completely handed her pleasures over to him, comfortable in her own skin and trusting him implicitly with her body. She might be inexperienced but damned if she wasn't the most sensual woman he'd ever been with.

"Tallulah," he whispered with effort.

She gave a soft sigh of contentment. "Yeah."

"I changed my mind." When confusion darkened her expression, he said, "I don't want you to keep your hands to yourself."

———

Wanting nothing more than to run her hands over his magnif-icent body, to kiss him all over and take his hard cock into her mouth so she could pleasure him in the same manner as he'd pleasured her, she tugged on his boxers. He quickly tore them off and everything in the way he responded to her seduction, to the way he stroked her with expertise, had her shedding all her inhibitions and enjoying this for what it was—one wild night of passion with a sexy soldier who knew his way around a woman's body. She was right about one thing, Garrett was definitely the guy to give her what she craved, what she'd been fantasizing about for far too long now.

Feeling bolder than she ever had in her life, and loving the effect her blatant seduction had on him, she pushed on his chest until he was flat out on the bed beside her, hers to do with as she pleased.

Truthfully, everything in what she was doing was unchar-acteristic of her. While she was uncertain at first, worried her seduction might make her look foolish, once she set things in to motion, bending over like Kat had suggested, there was no turning back. Perhaps the big city had changed her after all. Or perhaps there was something about this man, something about the hungry way he looked at her, lusted after her, touched her and kissed her, that made her feel bold, brazen. Wanton.

And she couldn't forget the way he encouraged her to show him what she wanted, never making her feel foolish at all. In fact, not only did he make her feel comfortable and sexy in the role of aggressor, he made her feel empowered. Damned if she didn't like that.

Either way, she was glad she pushed herself past her comfort zone and went for what she wanted. And who knew she could be so naughty, playing on their ruse to get him to touch her. A brilliant move on her part, she might add. Kat might have pointed her in the right direction but once she started down that path, and gave herself over to what she wanted, the rest came natural to her.

She climbed over him, her body already craving him again as she straddled him from above.

"And where do you suggest I put my hands?" she asked, loving this game they were playing.

He gripped her wrists and tugged until she was draped over him, her breasts crushed against his hard chest, her mouth inches from his.

"Everywhere," he murmured, need making his voice raspy.

Her mouth met his and she ran her hands through his mussed hair, then palmed his shoulders, taking immense pleasure in the feel of his muscled hardness. Between her legs she could feel his huge erection pressing against her wet seam, and her body vibrated, aching to feel him deep inside.

She broke the kiss and shimmied downward to feather her lips over his chest. Inhaling deeply, she breathed him in, savoring the clean scent of his recently showered skin. Her lips skimmed his stomach, and she could feel his cock pulse beneath her breasts.

She took his cock into her hands, lightly running her fingers over him. He groaned, a deep, guttural sound that prompted her in to action. She widened her lips to accommodate his girth, then inclined her head to feed his beautiful cock into her mouth, stopping when she could take no more.

His breath came in a rush, and she heard his throat work as he swallowed.

"Jesus Christ," he murmured as she began moving her head, sliding him in and out of her mouth. "That feels so fucking good."

He pitched forward when she lapped at the juices dripping from his crown, taking her time to savor every delectable drop.

She positioned herself over one of his legs, and began

moving, rocking, grinding her clit against him as her body burned up. Drinking in his saltiness, she moaned and worked her tongue over him. She rained kisses over his length, licking and sucking until his muscles bunched and clenched with the approach of release.

"You've got me right there, baby."

His hands gripped her head and followed the motion and she could feel the raw hunger, the urgency rising in him. Knowing he'd reached the point of no return, she slipped her hand lower to cup and massage his balls, then slid her tongue along the length of him, encouraging him to give himself over to the pleasure. His whole body trembled and taking her by surprise, he gripped her shoulders to pull her to him.

"I need to be inside you," he said a frantic edge to his voice. "Now." The intensity in his eyes when they met hers was as frightening as it was exciting.

Without waiting for her response he pushed her onto her back and widened her legs, taking full control of the situation. His nostrils flared as he reached for his wallet and pulled out a condom. After quickly sheathing himself, he climbed between her legs. He slipped a hand between them and stroked her pussy.

"Open for me, sweetheart."

Tallulah widened her legs even more, granting him better access. After nestling deep, he rubbed his cock along the length of her crevice before positioning it at her opening.

He lowered his body until the bulk of his weight was on her, and it occurred to her how much she liked being pinned beneath him. He gripped her hair, and his mouth found hers as his crown breached her opening. When their breaths mingled, she whimpered and moved restlessly, her actions telling him what she wanted.

"I need to take this slow," he growled, and she could sense

he was struggling to restrain himself as he pressed down harder on her body to still her.

Undeterred, she gyrated, and thrust her hips upward, driving him in another inch and hungering for him in ways that shocked her. "Maybe I don't want it slow."

"Jesus. If you keep that up I'll be done before I even begin, and you're not ready for me. Not yet." He slipped a hand between their bodies and stroked her clit to prepare her.

The touch of his deft finger on her engorged cleft nearly did her in. She moaned, and ran her hands over his back. "If you keep that up, I'll be done before we begin too."

The heat in his eyes licked over her. "Jesus, I love how wet you are for me."

She wrapped her legs around him and squeezed, forcing him in another inch. "That's because I'm desperate to feel you inside me."

"Fuck," he cursed, then squeezed his eyes like he was fighting an internal war, but when she said, "I want it hard," he pulled his cock out almost completely. For a moment she worried he was having second thoughts, then in one quick thrust he plunged deep, slamming her down on the bed and giving her what she asked for.

At that first sweet stab of pleasure a gasp ripped from her lungs and she wrapped her arms around him to hold on for the ride. He stayed still for a moment as his fullness stretched her apart, filling her in a ways she'd never been filled before.

She shifted, encouraging him to move and in no time at all he began pumping. Tallulah threaded her fingers through his hair, her body opening for him, eager for Garrett to take them both where they desperately needed to go.

"So good," she murmured as his groin pounded against hers. The crescendo of their union seared her nerve endings and somewhere in the back of her mind, some small part of her warned that after one night with him, she might never be the same again.

With his passion matching hers, he kissed her mouth hungrily and the heat in his eyes licked over her flesh as he burrowed deeper. She met each thrust, the sweet friction increasing the tension in her body.

She scraped her nails over him, never having experienced such raw need before. Honestly she was completely overwhelmed with the things this man made her feel, made her want.

Breathing labored, and moisture sealing their bodies together, he buried his face in her neck while one hand went to her aching breast. She arched into his touch, so delirious with pleasure she could barely see straight.

Passion peaking, she cried out, "I need, oh God, I need..."

Skilled in the art of lovemaking, and completely attuned with her needs, he angled his body for deeper thrusts, and her sex throbbed at the depth of penetration. Good Lord, the man certainly had a talent for knowing what she wanted, what her body craved. As he escalated the tension inside her, she concentrated on the points of pleasure. But soon the pressure in her body became too much to bear. She gulped air as fire zipped through her veins.

"Garrett," she cried with effort, then he slipped a hand between their damp bodies to stroke her, and a moment later a powerful explosion tore through her. Her pussy pulsed and spasmed, her sex muscles clenching him so hard, she practically locked him inside her.

He groaned and she could feel his muscles bunch, his cock throbbing with the need to peak. He moved his hips, drawing out her orgasm and she could tell how hard it was for him to hang on as he prolonged her pleasure.

When her body finally relaxed, she cupped his face, and pressed a kiss to his mouth. "Come for me."

He pressed down on her, and his nostrils flared as she shuddered in surrender. He pulled his cock all the way out, and then drove back inside, once, twice, and on the third time, he threw his head back and groaned.

As every muscle tensed, he dropped on top of her and she wrapped her legs around him tighter to hold him inside. She could feel his heart pounding as she squeezed her pussy muscles to help draw out his orgasm. By small degrees his body relaxed, sated and content from his own powerful orgasm.

He stayed inside her for a long time, then blew out a breath as he went up on his elbows to see her. A warm smile, so tender and sweet curled up his lips when their glances met, and Tallulah felt a strange little rush inside her. God, he looked so boyish and adorable with his hair mussed and moisture on his skin that she couldn't seem to tear her gaze away.

Once his cock grew flaccid, he pulled out and discarded the condom. After he settled back in next to her, she snuggled in close, thinking about how nice it felt to be held by him. She lifted her chin until their eyes met and found him watching her.

He brushed her hair from her face and in a voice that caressed her all over he said, "Jesus, that was…"

"A good start?" she teased.

"Yeah, a good start. You almost made me believe you liked it," he teased in return as his eyes fixed on her mouth, like he was about to kiss her again.

"Well I do what I can, you know, for the ruse." She gave a lazy cat-like stretch and inhaled, noting that the room was thick with the scent of their lovemaking. "At least now when you touch me I won't flinch."

His brow furrowed, real concern evident in his expression as he gave a slow shake of his head. "I'm not so certain about that."

Unease moved into her stomach and her pulse leapt as she went up on her elbows. "No? Why not?"

He looked thoughtful, contemplative for a moment. Then he touched her shoulder. With a small shove he pushed her back onto the bed, his voice full of mischief when he said, "Because I don't think I touched you everywhere."

"Oh." Her heart began pounding, excitement building inside her as she considered what he was saying, what he was suggesting. Playing along, she nodded her head in agreement. "That could be a problem."

"A very *big* problem."

She glanced down to see his cock thickening and her pulse jack-hammered. "A *big* problem indeed."

He dropped a soft kiss onto her mouth, a kiss so tender and gentle it took her by surprise. When he pulled back, he grabbed her hips and flipped her over. He threw his legs over hers and once he had her pinned beneath him, he gave her ass a light whack. She cried out in response, and he ran a soft palm over her cheek to soothe the sting he left behind.

"Do you think that covers it?" she somehow managed to ask, her muscles quaking and quivering in erotic delight.

"Nope, afraid not," he responded, running his fingers along her spine and splaying those big hands of his over her back.

"What are we going to do?"

"I suggest if we want to really pull this off, I'm going to have to make sure I've touched every inch of you. And I'm willing to spend the whole night doing just that and foregoing sleep if I have to."

"I wouldn't expect anything less from a dedicated soldier like yourself. You certainly seem like a hardcore military man who will do whatever it takes to get the job done."

"When I start something I like to see it through to completion."

"I do like a man of action, one who is dedicated to getting the job done."

He gave her ass another whack, then purposely put his mouth near her ear. In a soft, yet firm command, he said, "Good. Now get up on your knees."

 5

"**O**h. My. God."

"Shhh," Tallulah warned as Kat stood there wide eyed staring at her.

"Don't you dare shush me. I want all the details and I want them now," Kat said, planting her hands on her hips.

Grinning at her friend, Tallulah inched closer to the corner, moving out of ear shot as guests arrived at the hotel restaurant for the engagement party dinner.

"I already told you." Tallulah lifted her chin in defiance. "I don't kiss and tell."

"And I already told you that it's not the kissing I want to hear about," Kat retaliated, doing some weird head bobbing thing. "Now spill. Otherwise how do you expect me to live vicariously through you?"

"Okay, okay." Tallulah pulled Kat in closer as she laughed at her friend's antics. "Just quiet down before everyone hears you." She glanced around the wide expanse of room, looking at her family and friends who were all milling about and getting caught up in everyone's lives as they searched for their placement cards at the long, rectangular table. Her stomach fluttered when she found Garrett in the crowd, not that he was hard to find amongst her family, not with his height and powerful stature.

With his arms folded across his chest, the hardcore soldier looked like he just stepped off the cover of *GQ*. Dressed in a midnight suit that tapered to fit his muscular body to perfection, the man was every woman's fantasy. But underneath that suit she knew he was rugged and raw, a guy who oozed masculinity like none other. It was that masculinity that had her hormones playing a game of leapfrog and urging her to go for what she wanted, again and again.

Everything inside her reached out to him, and while she thought there might be awkwardness between them after indulging in a one-night stand, there was no discomfort to be found. For some reason it felt different with him. She'd been with men in her life, having been in a few committed relationships over the years, and even when she was devoted, afterward things were always uncomfortable. But with Garrett, there was warmth and familiarity, and everything in the way he looked at her, talked to her and touched her made the morning both comfortable and easy.

Beside him, her cousin, Andrew, who was a few years older than Tallulah, talked incessantly to Garrett as he cradled his three-month-old baby daughter, Sabrina, in his arms. Andrew's son, Jacob, ran around the room with his older sister, Cassie, and Tallulah felt a hitch in her heart, thinking what fun—not to mention how crazy—it would be to have three kids all under the age of five. Her hand went to her stomach and she wondered if someday she'd have a family of her own, or if she'd end up having surgery that would prevent her from having the children she longed for.

As though he felt her eyes on him, Garrett angled his head, and her knees nearly gave out at the intensity in his piercing blue eyes when they met hers. His eyes flared hot, and a slow lazy grin tugged at the corners of his mouth. As her body burned all over, her heart nearly stopped, forcing her to suck in a sharp breath to get it pumping up again.

"Holy shit," Kat said as her glance tennis balled between the two of them. "It must have been amazing."

Tallulah forced herself to tear her gaze away from Garrett and focus on her friend. "Amazing doesn't even begin to describe it," she whispered, unable to wipe the grin from her face, one that had been there since waking up a few hours ago. Not that she really slept. No, after round two, they'd showered together, which led to hot sex under the hot spray.

"He was that good, huh?"

"Yeah, he was."

"Please tell me you're going to do it again."

Tallulah gave her a mischievous smile, stole another glance at Garrett in time to see him scrub his hand over little Jacob's head, mussing up his hair, then arched a brow. "You mean the three times we did it isn't enough for you?" she asked, not that Tallulah thought it would be enough for her either. Heck, she was sure when it came to Garrett, nothing could sate her appetite.

"Three?" Kat pressed her palm to her forehead and sagged against the wall. "Oh, my God, I've created a nymphomaniac."

"Yes, I really should blame my naughty behavior all on you."

"Okay, it's official, I'm as jealous as hell." Kat shook her head. "And I'm definitely moving to Austin sooner rather than later. But seriously, Tallulah, you are going to do it again, right?"

"We never talked about it."

"Yeah." Kat nodded knowingly. "If I had him in my bed I wouldn't be talking either."

Tallulah narrowed her eyes. "Didn't you hook up with the best man? I saw the way you were eyeing him."

"No. I think I lost my touch."

Tallulah crinkled her nose. "Maybe he has a girl back home."

"Maybe." Then she winked and said, "But since Garrett is such an easy catch, more than willing to bed someone he barely knows, maybe I can have him for a round when you're finished."

Even though she knew her friend was teasing, an odd sensation gathered in her chest, a tightness that warned how easy it would be for her to get in over her head where Garrett was concerned.

"I...uh..." she began, but then Kat nudged her.

"I mean it's not like you're going to marry him."

"No, of course not."

Kat gestured with a nod. "I mean just look at him standing there sporting a sexy, bad-boy grin. He certainly doesn't look like the kind of guy who's in a hurry to settle down. If ever."

Tallulah caught his gaze again and she considered the way her pretend fiancé commanded a room, the way women gravitated toward him. Once again that strange feeling settled like a lump of oatmeal in her gut, and it took all her effort to push it down and remind herself this was simply a charade.

"No, you're right. He's not in a hurry to settle down," she agreed, hating that it bothered her so much. She had no claims on Garrett, nor did she want any. They were different people who wanted different things and were just doing each other a favor. Tallulah placed her hand on her stomach. "And he doesn't want kids."

Kat frowned and placed her hand over Tallulah's to give it a comforting squeeze. "How are you feeling? Any more pain?"

"I'm a little sore this morning."

"Yeah, but that's probably from all the great sex."

"Yeah," she agreed, but couldn't hide the worry on her face.

"Do you want me to take you to the doctor? We can stop at the clinic this afternoon before we go shopping for tonight's bridal party gifts."

"I'll be okay."

"Let's just play it by ear, then." She grabbed Tallulah's hand and gave a little tug. "Now come on, we need to get seated and it looks like your lover boy over there needs a break from Andrew. Jesus, that man never shuts up. I swear if I hear one more thing about gum disease or gingivitis I might have to kill myself."

"He sure has a captive audience in Garrett, doesn't he?"

Kat waved a dismissive hand. "Garrett should just blow him off."

Tallulah smiled, thinking it was sweet of Garrett to stand there and feign interest when her cousin was likely boring the hell out of him. She knew her soldier wasn't afraid of confrontation, but he was respectful when the situation called for it. Damned if she didn't like that about him.

Tallulah followed Kat across the room, and when she reached Garrett, he slipped his arm around her waist like touching her in such an intimate manner was the most natural thing in the world. And then, for what she could only assume was for show, he dropped a soft kiss onto her mouth, and lowered his voice before saying, "Save me."

Tallulah laughed, and glanced at her cousin. "Andrew," she began, and pointed to his young son on the other side of the room. "Jacob's putting his fingers in the chocolate fountain and then licking them. Isn't chocolate bad for the teeth?" Andrew gasped and called out to his wife, Cindy, before rushing across the room.

As she stood there admiring Garrett he blew a relieved

breath. Then angled his head, and gave her an odd look. "Everything okay?"

"Everything is fine."

"And Kat? She seemed pretty excited about something. Is she okay?"

"Just Kat being Kat," she said, not bothering to explain that she'd been telling her best friend how much he rocked her world last night—although she suspected he already knew she'd been kissing and telling.

Garrett straightened and looked past her shoulders. "There is someone you need to meet." Tallulah spotted a middle-aged woman coming their way, her sapphire-blue eyes mirroring Garrett's. She nodded, knowing exactly who she was. He put his mouth close to her ear. "You okay with this?"

Tallulah plastered on a wide smile as his mom stepped up to him. Garrett dropped a kiss onto his mother's cheek, then introduced the two. "Mom, this is Tallulah. Tallulah, this is my mother, Diane Andersen."

"Look at you," Diane said, pulling Tallulah into an embrace. "So pretty. And I've heard so much about you from Jenny and Ving that I feel like I know you already."

Tallulah blushed, instantly liking the woman who exuded such motherly warmth. Diane turned to Garrett and made a tsking sound. "You've got some explaining to do, young man. How dare you keep such a huge secret from us?"

"I wanted this time to be about Jenny." He gave his mom a sheepish look, but Tallulah couldn't help but feel a twinge of guilt. His mother was a sweetheart, and from the sparkle in her eyes when she looked at her son, it was clear how much she loved him. Honestly, when she agreed to this charade, she never really thought anyone would get hurt, but as she looked at his mother, she suddenly wasn't so sure anymore.

"I'm assuming when we return home you're going to bring her by the house so we can get to know each other better."

"Of course," he said.

Diane clapped her hands, a smile parting her rose-painted lips as she looked at Tallulah. "You'll be the first girl he's ever brought home. But since you're engaged, I'm guessing you'll also be the last."

Tallulah stole a sideways glance at Garrett, and speculated on why it pleased her immensely to learn that he'd never brought a girl home to meet his mother before.

"Now, let's have a look at that ring," Diane said, and Tallulah felt Garrett stiffen beside her. His mother took Tallulah's left hand in hers. She saw the silver band, and her sapphire eyes widened. Then an expression Tallulah couldn't identify crossed the pretty woman's face. She exhaled slowly and looked Tallulah straight in the eyes. "Very special. You're a very special woman indeed."

"Thank you." A little confused by her reactions, Tallulah twisted the ring on her finger, and made a mental note to examine it in more detail later.

"I'd better take my seat." Diane gave a little finger wave to a man across the room. "It looks like the luncheon is about to start."

"We'll catch up with you later, Mom. Tell Donovan I said hello," Garrett said, then turned his attention to Tallulah.

"I really like her." Tallulah glanced at the man his mother walked toward. She thought back to their plane conversation and remembered Garrett telling her that his father had passed away a few years ago, and she wondered about this new man in his mother's life. "Who's Donovan?"

"Bruce Donovan. He was my father's partner on the beat for years."

"And your mother's new one?"

"Something like that."

"I'm sorry, Garrett. Did I hit a sore spot?"

"No," he said. "I'm glad she's found someone. She

deserves to be happy and Donovan's a good guy."

Dropping the subject because it was clear that something about it bothered him, she said, "Your mom is going to be a wonderful mother-in-law."

"You mean for Ving, right?" he asked, arching a brow.

"Of course," she responded, understanding his insinuation. Then, to cover the strange sting she had no right to feel, she added, "Like I said, Garrett, you're not my type."

With that they moved toward the long table set for a family of forty. She reached for her chair, but taking her by surprise, Garrett pulled it out for her. She shot him a glance, enjoying this gentlemanly side of him. "Thanks," she said.

"My mother's watching and she would kick my ass if I didn't do right by you."

"She raised a gentleman."

He gave her a bad-boy grin. "She tried to."

He slipped in beside her and Andrew took the seat to his left as she shimmied close, craving the feel of him next to her. After last night there was a new intimacy between them, and when she caught her father looking at her, she suspected he sensed it too. For a moment she felt another twinge of guilt. She'd never lied to her folks before. Then again, she'd never stood up to them before, either.

Garrett put his hand on her thigh and she shivered under his touch. Her mind took that moment to revisit all the delicious things he'd done to her body last night, things she'd love for him to do again.

After everyone took their seats, Matt, Ving's best man, stood up, tapped his water glass, and proceeded to give a speech. All eyes turned to him while he told embarrassing stories about Ving, who looked like he was ready to crawl under the table.

The salads were served when Jenny's maid of honor stood and took her turn to captivate the audience, but Tallulah found it hard to concentrate with the way Garrett was drawing small circles on her inner thigh.

When the maid of honor told the story about how Jenny and Ving met, Garrett leaned in to her. His breath was hot on her neck and his eyes visually caressed her. "I forgot to tell you how beautiful you look."

She felt heat crawl up her neck. "Thanks. You clean up pretty nice yourself."

"The thing is…" He paused to rub her silk hem between his thumb and fingers and it was all she could do to stifle a needy moan. "I'm having a hard time concentrating, now that I know what you look like underneath this."

As they whispered intimately, quietly, someone at the head of the table cleared their throat. They both straightened in their chairs and when she caught Jenny staring at them, a wide smile on her face, Tallulah glanced around the table to find all eyes on them.

"Sorry," Tallulah rushed out, sinking in her chair and feeling like a school kid talking out of turn.

"Actually," Jenny said, calling them out. She cast Ving a glance then narrowed her focus on Garrett. "I have two very important men in my life and I want today to be about both of them."

Beside her Garrett flinched and if she wasn't mistaken he seemed to be avoiding Ving's direct glance. "What are you doing, Jenny?" he asked between clenched teeth.

"It's clear you two are crazy about each other," his sister responded, and Tallulah didn't miss the way Kat eyed her, or the way Garrett's best friend, Brad, glared at Garrett, a worried look on his face. "I think our families here would like to know a little about how this whirlwind engagement happened," she continued. "Maybe you could start by telling us all how you two met."

"Forget it," Garrett said and Tallulah could tell he was

uncomfortable, unable to come up with something on the spot. "This isn't about us," he growled.

"Come on, Garrett. I'm not letting you off the hook until you tell us how you managed to get a beautiful, *intelligent*, woman like Tallulah to fall for you," she teased.

"Did she lose a bet or something?" Ving called out, and laugher erupted around the table.

When Garrett opened his mouth and closed it again, she could feel his tension.

"Well," Tallulah began, coming to his rescue when the kids around the table gave her a ludicrous idea. "If you really must know."

Garrett nodded and she could sense his relief. "Yeah, we should let Tallulah tell it. She's a much better storyteller than I am."

Tallulah wiped her mouth with her napkin and took Garrett's hand into her own. "Garrett and I belong to the same health club and one day when I was teaching a ballet class, Garrett came rushing in." She smiled and said, "You see, his kick-boxing class is right after mine, and he had the times mixed up and thought he was running late." Everyone around the table nodded, and waited for her continue. She rolled her eyes. "But for those of you who know Garrett the way I know Garrett, you know how much he prides himself on *always* being right."

Rumbles of agreement erupted from around the table. "So you know he'd *never* admit to the mix up. He acted like he knew what he was doing all along and joined the class."

"Garrett joined your ballet class?" Jenny laughed. "Wow, what I would have done to see that show."

Tallulah patted his hand and he gifted her with a not-so-amused look. "Yeah, it was pretty special."

"Did you get him to wear the tutu?" the best man asked.

Just to make things interesting, she said, "Not at first, but when all the little girls surrounded him and demanded he wear one to fit in, he had no choice. And we all know *pink* is his favorite color." She exchanged a private knowing look with Garrett. "So we really didn't have to do much convincing."

Garrett sat there staring at her, his expression suggesting she was going to pay, and pay big time, for letting everyone around the table think he danced around the studio in a damn pink tutu.

She smiled at Garrett. "But seriously, those little girls were crazy about him and well, we all know Garrett has a soft spot for kids and wouldn't do anything to disappoint them."

The muscles in his jaw rippled as he clenched, but she continued anyway. "Of course, we had to piece a few of them together just to get one to fit properly. He's a little larger around the midsection than most of my four-year-olds."

When laughter broke out, Garrett cleared his throat and said, "Ah, that's not how I remember it at all, *Peaches*."

At the mention of her nickname, a shiver moved through her and she reminisced about all the ways he tasted her last night. She squeezed her thighs together, but it did nothing to take the edge off.

"Oh really?" Jenny folded her arms and she glared at her big brother. "Then why don't you tell us your version, Garrett? Not that any of us are going to believe you."

With that everyone started laughing and Garrett tossed his napkin on the table before saying, "What really happened was I was walking by and saw all these kids running around in complete chaos. You all know how much I hate disorder, and Tallulah seemed completely flustered so I thought I'd step in to help her. I mean, some of these kids are going to be our future soldiers. It's never too early to start disciplining them."

"Now that sounds like the Garrett I know," Ving said laughing. "But I'm still betting Tallulah's story was the truth."

"Thanks," Garrett said, as everyone else around the huge table began laughing and nodding in agreement with him. "Thanks a lot."

From across the table little Cassie started giggling. She jumped from her chair and began spinning around. "I want to wear a tutu. I want to take dance lessons."

"Me too," Jacob added, and then the two of them took off running.

Beside Garrett, Andrew exchanged an exasperated look with his wife who was about to go after them. "I got it," Andrew said, and turned to Garrett. Without giving Garrett a choice he thrust little Sabrina into his arms. "Here if you're so good with little girls, hold Sabrina for a second while I go round up the kids."

The second Tallulah saw Garrett with that sweet baby girl cradled next to his chest, his expression stricken as Sabrina broke out in a loud wail, her heart turned over in her chest and the room went a little fuzzy around the edges.

Her breath left her lungs in a rush and her stomach tumbled, because there was something so disarming, so damn adorable in the way he struggled to pacify the infant that she wondered what it would be like if *he* were her baby's father.

Except he didn't want children she reminded herself, and while the sex might have been fantastic, this thing between them wasn't real. She'd be wise to remember that.

"Get used to it," Ving called out. "I know my sister and she's going to want a brood someday."

"Tallulah," he whispered, his eyes pleading, his body stiff as he held the crying baby out to her. "I can't do this."

"Sure you can," she said.

"But she's so little."

Tallulah smiled. "Don't worry, she won't break." Instead of taking the baby from him, she adjusted the infant. "You just need to cradle her head in the crook of your arm." Once he shifted the baby, she said, "Now just rock her gently, like this." She mimicked the action, showing him how to do it.

He followed her directions exactly, and Sabrina instantly calmed down. Just then the wait staff came with their main courses, and conversation once again centered on the bride and groom. Except Tallulah was too enthralled in watching Garrett to pay much attention to what was being said, because when the little girl looked up at him, her big blue eyes damp from crying, tenderness stole over his face, the hard angles softening as his body relaxed. Tallulah's heart turned over in her chest. The man was full of virility and strength yet held that little girl in his arms with exquisite gentleness, a gentleness, she expected, he didn't even know he had in him.

The little girl's tiny hand curled around one of his big fingers, and her heart contracted as she watched it, the barrage of emotions catching her off guard and turning her inside out. She sat on her hands, because it was all she could do to keep them from shaking as she tried to compose herself.

God, he looked so adorable cradling that infant. She thought more about the man who said he wasn't father material as Sabrina settled in his arm, snuggling in like it was the most natural place in the world for her to be. She also thought about that scar on his face, and why he needed a pretend fiancée to land a job. The truth was she wanted to know more about this man. She wanted to know everything.

He turned and looked at her, the initial panic gone from his handsome face as he warmed to the baby in his arms, and need and desire surged through her veins in a way that frightened her. She inhaled sharply, and knew this was a dangerous game they were playing, because emotions played no part in this charade and if she wasn't careful, she feared she could fall for him.

6

Garrett rifled through his suitcase and grabbed a clean T-shirt. With his skin still damp from his shower, he struggled to pull it on as he glanced at all the boxes neatly stacked on the bed. "Do you think you bought Jenny enough gifts?"

"Some of them are from Kat too," Tallulah explained as she touched up her lips with gloss before tying a silk scarf around her neck. "Besides, I haven't been shopping with my best friend in ages so we just kind of went crazy."

"Kat seems very nice." He cocked his head, and took his time to peruse the beautiful woman before him. Warm familiarity moved through him when he thought about how easy she was to talk to, to be with. His glance moved to her sexy curves, and while he admired her in that knee-length, button-down coral dress that brought out the color in her eyes, he couldn't help but visualize her sexy body out of it. "She's very different from you."

Tallulah grabbed her purse off the dresser and dropped the tube of gloss inside. She smacked those sexy lips together and he couldn't help but remember how they'd felt wrapped around his cock. "Yeah, she's a real bad influence, that's for sure."

He stepped up to her, pulled her against him, and gifted her with an amused look. "Well I think I like the *advice* she's been giving you."

She flushed and Garrett brushed his finger along her cheek. "Do you have any idea how sexy you are when you blush?" Without giving her time to answer he dropped a quick kiss onto her mouth. "I like your family too. They're all very nice."

"You didn't find them a little loud, or a bit boring?" she asked, and he knew in an instant she was referring to her cousin, Andrew.

"Nah, it was only my mom, dad, Jenny and me growing up, so I kind of like the big group gatherings, and the open-door-policy thing you all have going on here."

"Speaking of gatherings, what time is the bachelor party?"

Garrett glanced at his watch and stepped back. "Two hours. I have some time to kill so I'll drop you off at your mom's for the bridal shower before I head over to the The Hop Yard."

She filled a bag with the presents, and slipped the handle over her arm. "I can make my own way there."

He feigned a shiver and thought about her overprotective mother. "Are you kidding me? Your mom would fillet me like a fish if I didn't escort you. She's pretty damn protective of you."

"So you noticed?"

"Oh, I noticed all right."

Tallulah laughed. "I guess you can see why I agreed to this charade."

"Because it's a whole lot easier than going to battle with her."

"She might actually convince me she knows what's best for me."

"And that would be staying here and marry Jason?"

She gave a disheartened nod.

"You don't want that, though, right?" he asked, needing in some strange way to hear her say it again, to know that she hadn't changed her mind. Not that it mattered to him. It didn't.

"No."

"You should never marry someone you don't love."

"I know."

He saw the miserable look on her face and something inside him softened. "It's only because she cares, you know."

"I know that too."

"She just needs to learn to let go. Maybe someday, when she sees you on the arm of the right guy, and she sees how happy you are then she'll come to understand that only *you* know what's best for *you*."

She pulled an apologetic face. "I'm pretty sure they don't think it's you."

"Hey," he said. "What's wrong with me?"

When she arched a brow that spoke volumes, he gave a sheepish grin. "Okay, never mind." He grabbed her hand and tugged. "Come on, let me take you to the bridal shower. Besides, if you show up alone it could raise suspicion."

"Yes, and that's the last thing we want to...*raise*."

Garrett shook his head, his cock thickening as this sweet and sexy girl teased him. "You keep that up and I'll never make it to Ving's bachelor party." As soon as he thought about Ving, the smile fell from his face.

"What's wrong?"

He shrugged and reached for his leather jacket.

"It's Ving isn't it?" she asked, and he noted the way her

gaze moved over his old worn jacket, pleasure in her eyes. "I noticed the way you kept avoiding his glance earlier."

"He's going to hand my ass back to me when this is all over." He shrugged his jacket on and ran his hands through his still damp hair. "We weren't supposed to sleep together."

"He doesn't have to know." She pulled a light cotton coat on over her dress. "Besides, who I sleep with is my business, not his."

"I know that." He pulled open the door and gestured for her to exit. "You're the only one who can make choices that are best for you." He wanted to say more, like even though he liked that she cared about other people's feelings maybe it was time to go to battle with her mother, or even Jason. But he shut his mouth instead, because he wasn't supposed to care.

"And why should he be upset, he's with Jenny." She poked him in the chest. "And she's *your* sister."

He rolled one shoulder and said, "They're engaged," like it explained everything.

"You can't tell me they didn't sleep together before they got engaged."

"No, but that's different, Tallulah. He cares about her. A lot. I knew it the first time he looked at her."

"Oh," was all she said as hurt registered on her face. Emotions passed over her eyes as she looked pointedly at the elevator, like it was the most interesting thing she'd ever seen. That's when he realized he'd hurt her, insinuating he didn't care about her at all.

Shit.

He backtracked. "What I'm trying to say is there is an unwritten rule amongst comrades, an honor in the brotherhood. We take care of each other's families; we don't sleep with them. Not unless we care...I mean, not when our intentions are less than honorable... Shit... I mean..."

She shook her head and when the elevator doors pinged open, she stepped on. "Sometimes you're not very good with words are you?"

He gave a helpless shrug. "I'm a man of action, remember."

"I remember." Her mischievous smile lightened the mood. "And I must say I do like that about you." He pressed the lobby button and when the doors closed she said, "Don't worry, Garrett. Ving never has to know we slept together. Your ass is safe."

He grinned. "Ooh, I do like it when you talk dirty."

"That will be our little secret too, just like sleeping together."

Garrett shook his head at her naivety, but loved her innocence just the same. "Are you kidding me? You don't think everyone at dinner this afternoon couldn't tell what we did last night. It was written all over our faces. Every time I looked at you all I could think about was hauling you up to our room again and having my way with you. Believe me, we were both easy reads."

Something passed over her face, a worried look, then she plastered on a smile as her glance fell over him. "Speaking of easy..."

He grabbed her and pinned her against the wall, and she gave a small gasp. "You've got something to say, Peaches."

"No, I don't believe so," she murmured, and moved against him, making his cock so hard he had no idea how he'd be able to walk off the elevator.

"Oh yeah, well I think you've always got something to say."

He pressed his lips to hers and her soft moan nearly did him in. Jesus he loved the way she responded to him.

A few minutes later, the elevator jolted to a halt and he inched back, putting a measure of distance between them before he got caught with his hands in the honey pot. In desperate need of fresh air, he slipped his arm around her back and hurried off.

Night had fallen when they exited the hotel, and Garrett called for a cab. They both climbed into the back and she relaxed into him, her warmth and scent doing traitorous things to his libido.

She gave the driver instructions, not that he needed them in a town where everyone knew everyone's business. Pushing back into the seat, she leaned into Garrett, her hands going to her stomach as a pained look came over her face.

"You okay?" he asked.

"Fine." She smiled, but he could tell it was forced.

He touched her chin until she looked at him. "What aren't you telling me?"

She crinkled her nose, and rubbed her stomach. "Just a bit of pain."

He straightened in his seat. "Pain? Why do you have pain?"

"Don't worry, Garrett. It's the endometriosis, and some-times I get bad cramps."

Worry moved through him. "It's not because of what we..."

"No, not at all," she assured him.

"Should we go to a clinic?"

"No," she said, giving him such a genuine smile his gut tightened in a strange way.

"There is nothing they can do. Don't worry. It will pass. Actually, it's almost gone now."

He opened his mouth to protest, but she leaned forward and pointed to her parents' house, which was alive with activ-ity. "Right there."

Garrett hopped from the cab. "Wait here, I'll be right

back," he said to the driver, then came around to help Tallulah from her side.

She accepted his hand. "You really are a gentleman."

He gave her a bad boy wink. "That's our little secret too," he whispered. When they reached the top landing of the stairs, he stopped and really looked at her. "Are you sure you're okay?"

She placed her hands on his chest. "I'm fine. Now go have some fun." She gave him a grin. "But not too much fun, otherwise Jenny might have something to say."

The front door flung open and Kat came rushing out. "Lu," she squealed, grabbing the bag of presents. "About time you got here."

Warmth and need unfurled inside Garrett's chest, producing an unfamiliar fullness when Tallulah's eyes lit, her smile so sweet and real as she hugged Kat. As the emotions caught him off guard, he suddenly wanted to take her back to the hotel so he could have her all to himself. Jesus, he couldn't believe he was actually jealous of her best friend.

Kat broke the hug and Tallulah went up on her toes to give Garrett a small kiss on the lips. "I'll see you soon."

Kat gave a knowing smile when he and Tallulah exchanged kisses, but it fell from her face as she looked past their shoulders.

"Oh shit."

Both Garrett and Tallulah spun around at the same time and when he spotted a man climbing from his car, an intense look on his face, Garrett stiffened, his body preparing for battle.

"I take it that's Jason," he said to Tallulah as she leaned in to him. When she nodded, Garrett felt his protective instincts come out full force. Anger washed the lust from his gut when he felt her tension. "I'll get rid of him."

With his speech slurred, Jason stormed toward them. "So

it's true then." His glassy eyes locked on Garrett. "You the guy everyone's talking about?"

"Yeah, I'm that guy." Garrett pulled Tallulah in closer.

Jason stumbled a bit, and held his hand out to her. "Come on, Lu. We had a pact."

"Jason," she murmured quietly. "You should go."

Jason made a step toward them, and Garrett matched it. "You heard the lady. You should go."

"So it's true then?" Jason asked, glaring at Garrett. "You're engaged?"

"That's right," Garrett said. "You've got a problem with that?"

Jason's nostrils flared. "Hell yeah, I do."

Tallulah's body tightened as the two squared off and Garrett cursed silently. While he wanted to punch the guy in the face, he'd never be disrespectful and cause a scene in front of Tallulah or her friends and family inside. Plus it wouldn't be a fair fight since the guy was shit-faced drunk.

"Okay, fine," he mumbled. "I'll let you have your fun with this guy until you get him out of your system. But when you're done slumming, you'll realize that I know what's best for you and that's when you'll come back home, to me."

Garrett took a threatening step forward. "Okay, time to back off, pal."

"We're not through, Lu," he said before stumbling backward.

"Yeah, you are." Garrett stormed toward the man's car. He pulled the keys from the ignition, and opened the cab door as the driver sat inside and silently watched the exchange. "You have two choices. You get in, or I make you get in."

Jason looked at him for a moment and wobbled on his feet. "You and me. We're gonna have it out," he said, and took a wild swing at Garrett.

Garrett easily dodged it and when Jason stumbled,

Garrett tossed him into the back seat of the car. Kat ran down the steps and gave the driver the address. Garrett slammed the door shut, then made his way back up the stairs to Tallulah.

He pulled her close and dropped a kiss onto her forehead. "You okay?"

"Yeah."

He ran his hands through her hair and held her head against his chest. He cursed under his breath, hating that everything about her made him want to care. "So that was Jason, huh?"

She nodded as the scent of his skin filled her nostrils. "He's upset."

"He's an asshole," he said working to tamp down his rage.

"He's drunk."

"Okay, he's a drunken asshole." Garrett held her shoulders and inched back. "I know it's not my business, Tallulah, and believe me I don't want it to be, but he just told you that you had no idea what was best for you, and was okay with you sleeping with me until you got slumming out of your system. That makes him an asshole in my books." Anger churned in his gut, and his nostrils flared. He put his mouth close to her ear and said, "Believe me, if this thing between us was real, I'd never tell you what to do, never cheat on you, and I'd never, ever share you with anyone. Not in a million years."

"You might be right, Garrett. Maybe he's not the guy I thought he was. Kat always said there was another side to him. Maybe I shouldn't be trying to protect his feelings."

"You're a considerate person." Dammit if he didn't love that about her. "And you really care about other people. That's not a bad thing, believe me. But I think sometimes people mistake your kindness and compassion for naivety." While Garrett appreciated that she cared about other people's feelings, he knew if she didn't speak her mind, she'd never be able to alter people's perception of her. Not that it was his business. It wasn't. And he wasn't about to say more and overstep his boundaries with her or her family.

"You're a real life hero, aren't you?"

He pulled back fast and gave a hard shake of his head. "I'm nobody's hero." Eyes perplexed she opened her mouth, but when the screen door behind them creaked open she shut it again. Garrett looked over her shoulders to see her mother, and her perceptive eyes widened when they locked on Garrett's.

"Is everything okay?" she asked.

"It's fine," Garrett said. "I was just taking care of..." He paused, looked back at Tallulah and said, "*Business*," putting extra emphasis on that one word to let her—but more importantly himself—know that what just transpired here was part of their business transaction. Part of the charade.

He handed Kat the keys to Jason's car when she came back and gave her a thankful nod as she ushered Tallulah inside. Since Tallulah's folks lived just on the outskirts of town, only a few miles from the city core, he decided to walk to the The Hop Yard. The fresh air would help him let off a little steam and figure out why it bothered him so much that Tallulah would even think about having a child with that asshole. He walked down the driveway and headed to the town's downtown core.

The road was dark, and not one car passed him on the way, the only noise cutting through the deafening quiet was the chorus of crickets moving about in the towering hills hugging the road. He drove his hands into his pockets and picked up his pace, but the sound of a woman's angry voice echoing in the still night stopped him cold. He glanced to his right and at the top of a winding driveway, floodlights came on and lit up the area with noon day brilliance. That's when he spotted the big old Victorian house, and a woman standing outside on the wraparound porch.

Without giving it another thought he took off running. When he reached the peak of the long driveway he noticed the elderly woman was dressed in nothing but her housecoat, a pellet gun in her hand.

Garrett stilled, and approached with caution. "Is everything okay?"

She waved her pellet gun as egg yolk and broken shells ran down the front of her house. "Those kids are up to mischief again."

"Shit," he heard from behind a woodpile haphazardly stacked near the garage. He turned toward it and when he spotted two kids running toward the road he bolted after them. He picked up pace, and lengthened his strides, but Jesus they were fast. At the end of the driveway, he finally closed the distance and caught one kid by the scruff of the neck. He lifted him clear off the ground, his feet flailing helplessly. The kid, who looked to be about thirteen, struggled valiantly, but couldn't break free of Garrett's firm hold.

"Jimmy," he called, his pubescent voice rising an octave. "Jimmy, shit. Get him off me."

Jimmy stepped from the dark, but when he caught sight of Garrett, who towered over the boys, he shrank a little.

"Come on, let him go. We were just having a little fun with old lady Henderson," he said.

"You think scaring an old lady and egging her house is fun?" Garrett let the kid go, and nudged him toward the house. "Let's go, and don't even think about running again."

The kids stumbled a little. "Where?"

"Where do you think?"

"You're not going to call the cops on us are you?"

Garrett didn't feel the need to involve the law. Christ, they were just bored kids doing what bored kids do. It wasn't like he had never delved into mischief when he was a teen. But it didn't mean he wasn't going to teach them a lesson.

He scowled and said, "When I'm done with you you're going to wish I had."

"Shit." Jimmy grudgingly walked toward the house.

Garrett marched them up the steps, and Mrs. Henderson glared at them. "Well if it isn't Jimmy and Kent Tanner." She shook her head. "I should have known. Your papa is going to give you both an ass whipping when he finds out."

"Please don't tell him," they both said, eyes wide and fearful.

The old screen door creaked as Mrs. Henderson stepped behind it, propping her gun on the doorframe just inside.

Garrett folded his arms, and gestured toward the egg. "Clean it up."

When the one named Kent gave him a defiant look, Garrett stepped up to him and put on his best hard-ass face. "You have two choices, you either clean it up, or I borrow that gun from Mrs. Henderson and practice my shot." He went silent for a moment, to give more impact to his words when he added, "And I'm a pretty damn good shot already."

The kid swallowed. "Shit," he said, and Mrs. Henderson disappeared inside. Garrett could hear water running from inside the house. She came back out with paper towels, two sponges, and a bucket full of sudsy water.

Garrett stood there, arms folded as he watched the boys reluctantly take it from her. Then he glanced around the property, taking note of its run down condition. "I think you boys need to find something productive to do with all that extra energy you seem to have."

With his sponge poised over the bucket, Kent glared at him.

"Mrs. Henderson can use a hand around this place. I

expect you both here tomorrow to take care of the lawn, and that woodpile."

"Ah, come on."

"Where's that gun?" he asked Mrs. Henderson, who was hovering just inside the door.

"Shit," Jimmy said.

Keeping the grin from his face as the kids went back to cleaning, he stepped inside the house to speak quietly to Mrs. Henderson. The scent of warm gingerbread filled his senses and reminded him of home and hearth as she beamed up at him, her cloudy brown eyes narrowing with careful regard. "You're that young man I've been hearing so much about, aren't you? The one that's keeping Tallulah from moving back home." She shuffled across the room, grabbed a tin off her counter and held it to him.

"I'm not keeping Tallulah from doing anything." The sweet smell of spices and sugar reached his nostrils and he peered into the container. "She's a grown woman who makes her own choices."

She eyed him. "You weren't really going to practice your shot were you?"

He grinned and accepted a cookie. "Sure I was."

She laughed. "Are you a lawman?"

"No, ma'am."

"Well you should be. You got a way with delinquent kids. Look at them out there; you scared them straight."

"If they give you any more trouble you just let me know." He winked and said, "I've been feeling a little trigger happy lately."

Mrs. Henderson smiled. "You're a nice young man. Barbara and George got nothing to worry about with you. You'll take good care of that girl of theirs." She scowled. "I never was too fussy about that Jason fella, anyway."

Garrett finished his cookie and she tried to give him

another. "I'm good, thanks." He jerked his thumb toward the kids outside. "But I think those two might like a couple when they're done."

She snarled, but said, "I suppose you're right."

Garrett went back outside and stayed until the boys finished cleaning, then when they were done, Mrs. Henderson plunked herself down on her wooden bench and opened her tin for them. While they munched, she began talking, and their eyes widened with genuine interest when she began telling them stories of her own youth, and the things they did for fun.

With that Garrett retraced his steps down her long driveway and began his trek back to town. He pushed through the doors of the pub and since he was still a bit early, he grabbed a stool at the bar. He ordered a beer, and as he nursed it, Brad took the stool beside him.

"Hey," Garrett said, and gestured the bartender to bring two more brews.

Brad tossed a handful of nuts into his mouth. "I heard what happened."

Garrett turned to him. "What are you talking about?"

"The fight you had with Tallulah's ex."

Surprised at how fast news spread, he said, "There was no fight."

"That's not the way I heard it."

"Then you heard it wrong. The guy was drunk. I sent him home in a cab."

"Ah, now that makes more sense. I've never seen you fight just to fight. I knew the rumor had to be wrong because the Garrett I know only goes to battle when he's got something to fight for."

Garrett took that moment to think about how much he wanted to pummel Jason for disrespecting Tallulah and her family, but he wasn't about to cause a scene at his sister's bridal shower. Plus, Tallulah was upset enough as it was. He wasn't going to add to it.

Beside him Brad remained quiet, too quiet, and since his best friend had an opinion on everything, it made Garrett uncomfortable. "You got something to say, Brad?"

"No." He chuckled and said, "I was just thinking about that little speech Tallulah gave at dinner."

Garrett tossed a peanut into his mouth and chewed. "She's quick on her feet."

"I'd say she knows you better than you think."

Striving for normalcy, he rubbed his temple and explained, "Yeah, well she got some things wrong."

"Really, and here I think she got everything right."

"Then you'd be wrong."

"So this thing between you two, it's just pretend? Because I saw the way you were looking at her."

"It's an act, Brad. A charade. We had a room full of people we had to convince we were lovers."

"Fine," he said, sounding unconvinced. He took a huge swig of beer, and rolled the bottle his palms. "Since you're not a real couple when this *charade* is over maybe I'll go for it with her. A sweet thing like her could really make a man change his ways."

Something dark and dangerous rumbled inside Garrett's gut. "Stay the fuck away from her."

Brad set his bottle onto the countertop, patted Garrett on the shoulder and with a wry grin on his face said, "Yeah, pal, it's real clear that she means nothing to you."

As his words hit like a round of mortar, Garrett dropped his empty bottle on the bar top and gestured for another.

He drained half the beer in one gulp, and tried not to think about Tallulah, or how she was getting under his skin. Ving and the rest of the guys came through the front door, interrupting his thoughts, and soon he was lost in drinking games and good old camaraderie amongst comrades.

Halfway through the night a stripper came from the back room, and cheers erupted around him. While he always enjoyed a good show, he couldn't seem to focus on anything besides Tallulah, couldn't help but think how every other woman paled in comparison.

"Hey, how about a lap dance for the groom?" Matt shouted out, and the pretty girl with next to nothing on shimmied up to Ving.

Ving laughed, shook his head, and held his hands up palms out. "No way, man. Jenny would kill me. I can look but I can't touch."

"Then how about you, Garrett?" Matt said. "Since you're the next guy on the chopping block."

Garrett tried to smile, tried to loosen the knot that had taken up permanent residency in his gut, and shook his head. "Sorry," he said. "I only have eyes—" he stopped to wiggle his fingers, before adding, "—and hands, for Tallulah."

He caught Ving's glance and when the man gave a nod, guilt swamped him.

Shit.

As the party went on Garrett knocked back another beer, but the alcohol did little to relax him. Even though it was a bad idea, all he wanted was to make his way back to the hotel, to Tallulah.

At least the wedding was in a couple of days, and Sunday evening, the day after the ceremony, he'd be returning to Austin. Once his feet were on familiar ground he'd be able to get her out of his system and get his mind back on his work and off all the things he suddenly found himself wanting, but could never have.

A short while later, once the party ended, they all climbed into a cab and made their way back to the hotel. He took the elevator to his floor, and wondered if Tallulah would be awake. Perhaps he'd get lucky and she'd be sound asleep, then he wouldn't be tempted to take her again.

He slipped inside and the warmth of the room fell over him as his eyes adjusted to the dim light. A movement near the window drew his attention and lust hit like a high voltage jolt as Tallulah perched on the edge of the sill, her sweet scent permeating the room.

"Hi," she said, her voice low, seductive as the moonlight spilled over her.

He shrugged out of his jacket and pitched his voice low to match hers. "What are you still doing up?"

"I wanted to wait up for you. Just to make sure you made it back okay."

His gut tightened because this felt real, too real. Too good.

She started toward him, her movements seductive, purposeful. "Did you have a nice time tonight?" he asked struggling for small talk when all he wanted to do was drag her into his arms.

"I did." She came closer, her nearness making him breathless. "Jenny loved all our gifts."

"Our gifts?"

She placed her hand on his chest and smiled at him. "I put them from you too, Garrett. That's what couples do."

Everything in the way she said couple and lumped them into the same category made him forget this was pretend. Unease moved through his bloodstream, but when he caught the longing in her eyes, it was quickly forgotten. He glanced downward and his cock twitched, possessiveness raging through him when he glimpsed her pretty pink negligee and matching panties.

His blood pulsed hot, and he struggled to rein in his lust. "You look beautiful."

"What, this old thing?" Her soft laugh curled around him and settled deep in his groin.

He ran his hand along her arm and brushed her hair from her shoulder. That's when he saw the price tag at the back. His chest tightened and a low growl rumbled in his throat.

"You..." He stopped to swallow. "You did this just for me?"

His heart skipped a beat and even though it might not be in his best interest, because he definitely didn't want to develop more than casual feelings, he knew he had to have her again.

"I found it in the bottom of my suitcase." She blinked dark lashes over not so innocent eyes. "And look at that, it just happens to be your favorite color." Her fingers curled in his shirt and the passion in her eyes became his undoing.

"You didn't have to do this. Not for me," he said, but was touched deeply that she had. Garrett gripped the price tag and with one quick tug he tore it free.

"Oh," she said when he discarded it, her eyes conveying her embarrassment as she looked away.

He cupped her chin and turned her face until she was looking at him. "Don't, Tallulah. Don't ever be embarrassed with me," he said and when her breathing grew shallow, he began sweating. Christ, no woman had ever made him sweat before.

Feeling a little shaky, a little unstable, he backed her up, and grabbed the scarf off the bed. His mind raced through all the events since they'd landed in town, from his meeting with her folks, the luncheon and the bachelor party, to his run-in with her ex. Honestly, he hated how everyone wanted to steer her life. Then again, they all thought they knew what was best because in order to make them happy, she never gave voice to what she really wanted.

He might not have known Tallulah very long, but being with her and watching her for the last couple of days made it feel like he'd known her forever. Made him want to do things for her. Made him wish he were the man she thought he was.

"Garrett?" she asked, after he'd gone quiet.

"Yeah?"

"Are you okay?"

He exhaled slowly, and even though he feared he'd never be okay again, he said, "Yeah, I'm okay." He brushed his thumb over her mouth, and while emotions played no part in this charade, he knew what he was about to do next was as much for her as it was him.

You're not supposed to care.

"Do you trust me?" he asked and moved his thumb to her flushed cheek, thinking about how perfect she was, and how she was good with her words, but needed to learn to use them to tell people what she wanted.

She nodded without hesitation, and tenderness stole over him. Working to still his shaky hands, he grabbed her arms and pinned them at her back. He buried his face in her hair and inhaled her scent as he shackled her wrists, binding her hands tightly with the scarf.

"What are you doing?" she asked breathlessly, her eyes wide and her body quaking beneath his touch.

He stepped away for a moment and grabbed another scarf from her open suitcase. He cupped her face, and looked directly into her eyes.

"Garrett," she murmured, leaning into his touch, those dark expressive eyes of her so honest, so full of trust that it stole his next breath.

He gave a little push. When she dropped to the bed, he sank to his knees in front of her and climbed in between her thighs. "I'm a man of action, and you're a woman of words, Tallulah," he whispered into her ear. "And now I'm going to make you use them."

7

He sent her a look so potent it touched something deep inside her, something she feared there was no coming back from as he brushed the scarf over her cheek. Her heart rated quickened, the cool, smooth texture of silk against her skin eliciting a shiver as she waited to see what he'd do next. Taking her by surprise, he covered her eyes, and when he knotted the scarf behind her head, she sat there trying to remember how to breathe.

"That's not too tight, is it?" he asked, his low voice doing mysterious things to her body and soul.

"No," she whispered as equal amounts of excitement and alarm hit at the same time. Never in her life had she been tied and blindfolded, although she had to admit, it felt highly erotic, completely freeing—and not something she'd do with just anyone.

With her other senses finely tuned, she listened as Garrett shuffled between her legs. She took that moment to wonder exactly what he was up to and what he meant when he said she'd be using her words.

"Garrett," she said, pulling his scent into her lungs and catching the tang of beer on his breath.

"Yeah?" he asked, and she noted how his voice sounded deeper when she couldn't see him. She reached out to touch him but remembered her hands were tied.

"What are we doing?"

Instead of answering he asked a question of his own, "Are you comfortable, sweetheart?" She heard a new tenderness in his tone and assumed the beer had mellowed him.

She nodded as a slow tremor worked its way through her blood.

His hand went to the straps on her negligee and he ran his fingers up and down them, then he lightly brushed the peaks of her nipples. Ripples of sensual pleasure coursed through her and her pulse kicked up a notch as she leaned into his touch.

He pulled his hand away, and she gave a low growl of displeasure, instantly missing his heat, the feel of his rough palms on her body.

"Do you want me to touch you, Peaches?" he asked and she could sense him backing away, putting distance between them.

Aching to lose herself in him, she nodded, needing in the most frightening ways to feel him on top of her, inside her.

"Then tell me. Tell me exactly what you want and I'll do it."

Her heart leapt because while she'd been bold last night, showing him what she wanted, never had she *told* a man what she wanted before. Heck, she'd never even used anything but technical terms for her private parts before.

Suddenly unsure, she began, "Garrett..."

"Tell me, Peaches," he pushed. "Tell me where you want my mouth, my hands, my cock."

She swallowed hard, and thought more about this game he

was playing, how he was pushing her beyond her comfort zone, and how he'd just told her never to be embarrassed with him.

Honestly, she'd be a fool not to shed all her inhibitions and enjoy every moment she could with him, before they returned to Austin, to reality.

"Tell me," he said again, his tone a little firmer, his presence overwhelming her even with her blindfold on.

She lifted her chin and wet her lips, the warmth of the room engulfing her. "I want you to kiss me."

She felt his hands on her thighs, and listened to his lusty groan as he spread them wide to climb in between. Her sex moistened as he pressed against her, and when she felt how aroused he was, she shifted granting him better access.

His mouth brushed hers, soft at first, then harder, more demanding. He lightly bit her bottom lip and she gasped. But he swallowed the sound, and deepened the kiss until she was damn near delirious with want.

He inched back, his mouth still hovering over hers. She licked her lips and said, "I love the way you kiss me."

"Where do you want my mouth now?"

"My neck," she murmured without hesitation, and thought she heard Garrett give a needy sigh of acquiescence.

He pushed her hair off her shoulders and abandoned her mouth. She sat still, her senses tuned as he traced the pattern of her face, and surfed his fingers along the outline of her jaw, his touch so gentle and tender, it caught her off guard. Warmth flooded her, and she drew a shaky breath as she absorbed his heat.

A second later he buried his face in her neck. His tongue felt so gloriously erotic on her flesh her throat dried and a new kind of hunger consumed her. She struggled with the binding on her hands, wanting to push his head lower, to show him where she wanted his mouth, but couldn't loosen the knot.

"Lower," she murmured, thrusting her pelvis forward to force his arousal to press harder against her drenched sex. "Lower, please..."

He put his mouth at the base of her throat and his breath tickled her flesh. "Do you mean here?"

"No," she cried out.

"What about here?" her asked, and ran his lips and teeth over her shoulders.

A quiver moved through her, and with her patience at an end she blurted out, "My breasts."

He pulled back and her skin chilled where his hot mouth had just been. "What do you want me to do to your breasts?" he asked.

She growled in frustration. "Please, I want you to take them into your mouth. I want you to lick and suck my nipples. I want you to...*bite them*."

"That's a girl." He ran his palm over the curve of her breasts before he tugged the negligee down to free her aching breasts. His lips scorched her skin when he pulled one breast into his mouth, and when she arched into his kisses, a primal sound rumbled in the depths of his throat, making her feel bolder, more confident in what they were doing.

"Bite me." Her body quivered in delight and her thighs hugged his hips, afraid he'd stop at any moment.

He clenched hard, and when she let loose a cry of ecstasy, his moans of pleasure merged with hers. The soft blade of his tongue soothed the sting he left behind, and warmth brewed deep inside her.

He spent a long time licking, sucking and nibbling, until languorous warmth stole over her and small spasms pulled at her core. She gave a needy, not quite satisfied sigh, her body trembling all over. Good God, the pleasure was exquisite but this slow seduction was about to become her undoing. Needing him to touch her everywhere, to bury his mouth in the apex of her legs, she widened her thighs, letting him know in no uncertain terms what she wanted.

"I need..." she murmured, as her body burned from the inside out.

"What do you need?" he asked, his voice stroking her all over.

Acutely aware that he was forcing her to say the words, to tell him exactly what she wanted even though coherent thought was nearly beyond her, she whispered with effort, "I need you between my legs. I need to feel your tongue on me."

"Where on you?"

Her heart missed a beat. "On my pussy."

His mouth skinned downward, dancing over her thin negligee as his fingers lightly massaged the skin above her midriff. Then he pulled back, and gripped her thighs. He never spoke for a long time and she could sense him looking at her. It filled her with excitement, and a longing so deep and profound it made her feel a bit uneasy. Before she could examine it further, or remind herself they weren't playing for keeps, he dipped a finger under the small fabric covering her sex, and pulled it to the side to expose her hot core.

He sucked in a sharp breath, the sound curling around her. "Fuck," he murmured and she could hear the need, the impatience in his voice.

The scent of her arousal saturated the small room and teased her nostrils. A shiver tingled all the way to her toes as her blood pulsed hot.

"Jesus," he murmured, desire deepening his voice and fueling the need inside her.

Her sex pulsed at the warm and wicked sensations. Unable to hold back any longer, she said, "I need your mouth on me. I need you to put your tongue on my clit, and your fingers inside my pussy. I need you to make me come."

She heard his throat work as he removed her panties, and a second later his mouth pressed hungrily to her sex, his tongue toying with her inflamed clit while his fingers breached her drenched opening. He pushed one inside, and she clenched around him, his touch sending shockwaves through her. She moved against him, rocking her hips and savoring everything he offered.

Beneath his artful manipulation, heat rushed through her and her orgasm was so close she could barely think straight. She began panting as his mouth pillaged her with fierce hunger, his finger brushing her inner core until her nerve endings were on fire.

He gave long, thrusting strokes, and her heart hammered when he deepened the kiss, the sweet torment taking her higher than she'd ever been before. She felt the tension of an impending orgasm and let her head roll back, wanting nothing more than to forget the real world and just ride the glorious waves forever and ever. Heat reverberated through her blood and in no time at all her body went up in a burst of flames. Her orgasm hit so hard, it knocked her off balance.

She pulsed and throbbed and cried out his name as he put his arms around her hips to hold her as he lapped at her cream, his tongue prolonging the release.

"You are the sweetest thing I've ever tasted," he murmured from deep between her legs.

She rolled her tongue around her dry mouth and worked to swallow. "Let me taste," she said quietly, and felt a little jolt of pleasure when air rushed from his lungs, followed by a strangled cry. A second later he shifted positions, and she warmed at the intimacy in what they were doing when he captured her mouth in a slow, simmering kiss. He growled, and sexual prowess rolled through her to know she could pull such a fierce reaction from him.

She moaned as she tasted herself on his mouth. "Mmm, peaches," she managed to get out between his heated kisses and felt his body stiffen.

"Do you have any idea what you're doing to me?"

He pressed his lips to hers again, except this time his burning mouth came down hard, his kisses frantic, urgent.

He kissed her for a long time, and as she savored the flavor of his mouth, her sex began throbbing once again, needing him inside her. "Garrett," she said hardly able to breathe let alone speak.

He ran his hands through her hair. "What is it, Peaches?" His voice wavered, and she could tell he was struggling for control as his body clamored for attention.

"Stand up."

"Why?"

"Hey, I'm the one who's supposed to be doing the talking, you're the man of actions, remember."

"Christ," he said, and she could just picture his sexy smile. "What have I done to you?"

"Maybe you should be thinking about what I'm going to be doing to you," she teased.

His soft chuckle curled around her and she listened to his clothes rustle as he obeyed her command. "I'm standing," he said.

"Unbutton your pants. I want to taste you."

"Jesus Christ." He gripped her head. "Tallulah..."

"Do it," she demanded. "Take off your pants and put your cock in my mouth."

———

Garrett could barely think, let alone work his zipper. As he watched Tallulah blossom before his eyes he ached to tear that sexy negligee from her body and drive into her so hard and deep they'd both forget what century they were in.

Working to keep his hand from shaking, he released his zipper. The sound cut through the air as she sat there perched on the edge of the bed, her mouth poised open, waiting for his cock.

Sweet fuck!

His skin grew tight and his body thrummed and he had no idea how he'd ever be able to last. One flick of that hot tongue, one long suck and he'd be shooting off in the back of her throat. But he didn't want to come in her mouth, he wanted to be deep inside her, wanted to join them as one when he gave himself over. He groaned as he made short work of his clothes, tossing them to the floor in a forgotten heap.

With her hands still tied, she widened her mouth, and he walked up to her. His cock brushed against the side of her face and she moaned. He gripped the base of his erection and positioned his crown near her lips.

"You've got me so fucking hard, sweetheart," he said in a low, barely controlled voice.

She leaned forward and wrapped her pretty lips around him, and he threw his head back, sure he'd died and gone to heaven. She rocked against him, pulling him in as far as she could, her teeth scraping over his engorged shaft. Her sexy mouth was so goddamn hot he knew he was going to pass the finish line in record time.

Her dark curls fell over her shoulders, and he brushed them back so he could watch her take him into her mouth. It was the most erotic thing he'd ever seen. Her hot pink tongue worked magic on his shaft. She dragged it over him and the moisture left behind glistened in the moonlight. Women had sucked him before, but there was something so intimate in the way she pleasured him, his mind traveled a path he knew he couldn't walk, considering they both wanted different things in life.

His thoughts scattered when she moaned in bliss, letting him know how much she liked what she was doing. Jesus. Frantic with the need to be inside her, to feel her tight walls wrapped around his cock, he gripped his dick, drove in to her mouth a few more times then pulled completely out.

Shaken by how much he needed her, his hands went to her negligee and he fumbled with the tiny buttons. Deciding he was too far gone to properly work his shaky fingers, he gripped the fabric and tugged, listening as the buttons scattered to the floor. She gasped, her chest heaving in a way that would drive a sane person mad.

As her aroused scent impregnated the sheets, his throat tightened. "I need to fuck you."

"Garrett," she said breathlessly. "I need to see you."

He pulled the scarf free and caught the way she looked at him. His heart hammered and he released her hands, desperate to feel them on his body.

No longer able to fight the inevitable, he said, "I want you on your knees. Now."

Without a moment's hesitation, she crawled over the mattress, and when she put her sweet ass in the air, it became difficult to think. Restless and edgy he kneeled on the bed and came up behind her. He ran his hands over her soft contours, reveling in the feel of her skin and loving the way her body opened for him.

He pushed one finger inside her and found her so fucking wet he began trembling from head to toe. "Tallulah," he murmured, astonished by the need she raised in him.

"Please..." she said in return, her voice rough with desire as she wiggled her backside.

He swallowed. Hard. Frantic and damn near crazed to be inside her he growled, "I want you so much."

"I want you too."

He positioned his cock at her entrance. Baser instincts took over and he forgot every sane thought and drove into her. Tallulah clawed at the mattress and Garrett growled furiously in response.

He gripped her hips for leverage and pushed impossibly deeper, needing to bury every inch of himself inside her, including his balls. Warm and wanting she moved against him, and he could feel himself twisting up inside, the emotions she roused in him were completely disconcerting.

"So good. So fucking good," he murmured, his pulse beating madly at the base of his throat as flames licked over him. His balls slapped against her and the air around them crackled, the tension of his orgasm tightening his muscles. He leaned over her, and dipped a hand between her legs.

He stroked her clit, and she cried out. A second later she clenched around him, her pussy gripping his cock so damn hard he could barely hang on. Blinding pressure built inside him then he quickly joined her in orgasm, spilling himself inside her and giving every inch of himself. His body strained, his orgasm so powerful and intense, he began trembling, panting, gasping for his next breath.

They stayed like that for a long time, his cock buried deep in her body, like it's where it always belonged. He listened to her breathe, and by small degrees he relaxed against her. He ran his hands along her silky back, and she shivered when he pulled out of her. They collapsed on the bed and he grabbed her and pulled her to him. Once she snuggled in close, contentment written all over his face, he made a move to discard the condom. That's when he realized he hadn't worn one.

"Oh fuck."

Tallulah tightened beside him and tipped her head. Big brown eyes blinked up at him. "What?"

"We didn't use a condom." He shook his head. "Oh fuck, fuck, fuck. What was I thinking?" he rushed out, but it was a question he already knew the answer to. He wasn't thinking. At least not with the head on his shoulders. "Shit, I always use a condom." He brushed her hair from her face and when he saw concern backlighting her eyes his heart twisted. "I'm clean. You don't have to worry about that. But what about…?"

"I'm clean too," she assured him.

He smiled at her, and stopped to rub his hand over her stomach. "I know you are, but that's not what I was talking about."

"Oh," she said. "I'm on the pill."

"Why are you on the pill if you want to have a baby?"

"My periods are irregular because of the endometriosis and the pill helps regulate them." Then with a slight shrug she added, "My chances of concceiving are slim anyway, even if I wasn't on it."

"We still shouldn't take chances," he said. "I won't let it happen again."

She nodded in agreement, then after a long thoughtful moment she gave him a warm smile. "It's kind of nice, actually."

"Nice?"

She shrugged. "I don't know. I guess I just mean it was a first for both of us. Something that can just be ours, know what I mean?" When he didn't say anything she looked a little embarrassed and said, "Maybe I'm just being silly."

"It's not silly," he assured her, completely unprepared for the things this woman made him feel. But they were different people, who wanted different things he reminded himself.

And none of this was real.

She settled back in the crook of his arm, her hair

tumbling in disarray over his shoulders, making her look so sexy and desirable. Garrett knew any man would be lucky to have her. She'd be the perfect mother, the perfect wife. She just needed to find the right guy.

After a long time he said, "I'm sorry."

"What are you sorry for?"

"I know how much you want a baby. I could see it in your eyes when I was holding Sabrina."

She snuggled into him and he flinched when she rubbed the scar on his cheek. "I'm praying for a miracle."

He tried to breathe normally and hoped she couldn't hear the pounding of his heart. "Oh yeah?"

"Sure. I had a cousin who was married to a guy for years. She had the same problem as me and couldn't conceive. They ended up divorced, because he said she was broken and couldn't give him the family he wanted. She met another guy and within months they were pregnant."

"Her ex sounds like an ass."

"Yeah, and I think it was nature's way of saying she was with the wrong guy. So when she did find Mr. Right, she got the baby she wanted."

As he thought about Tallulah with another man, her Mr. Right, his chest tightened with jealousy. Which was ridiculous, really. He had no right to be jealous and she deserved to have everything she wanted.

She toyed with the ring he'd put on her finger. "Garrett?"

"Yeah?"

"Why do you need a pretend fiancée to get a job back home?"

He stiffened, but relaxed as she began marching her fingers over his stomach. "They think I'm scarred," he admitted, and then realized how easy it was to tell her, to talk to her, how strangely good it felt to share that painful truth with her, even though he knew they shouldn't be dipping into personal territory.

She touched the crescent mark on his face again. "Scarred?"

"Yeah. Scarred. As in emotionally damaged."

"Does it have something to do with this?"

He grabbed her hand and held it. "I guess."

"Did this happen on tour?"

"Yeah."

"What exactly is this job you're after?"

"Head of a new security alarm response team in Austin's business district."

"It must be very important to you if you're going through the trouble of a fake engagement." When he shrugged, she frowned. "It doesn't sound like it's your dream job."

"It's a job."

"Becoming director at the daycare is my dream job. Well, actually opening my own center someday is my real goal. I love working with kids, but some real changes need to be made on the business and government side of things."

"Oh yeah? Tell me about it," he said, as her eyes lit with excitement and deterred her questions about his personal life.

"I'm really interested in working on a new curriculum for the kids, new nutritional menus and advanced training for the teachers." She exhaled slowly. "I wish my folks could see how important it was to me. My mom wants me to follow in her footsteps and be a stay-at-home mom. Not that there is anything wrong with that, I just want different things."

Garrett turned on his side and propped his head on his elbow. "You know," he began slowly as he brushed her hair from her face. "I love how thoughtful you are. It's one of the things that separates you from most women I know. It's understandable that your mother wants you to follow in her footsteps, because she's had a happy life, but sometimes you have to go to battle for what you want."

She nodded and said, "Did your father want you to follow in his footsteps?"

He dropped back down onto the pillow, and his heart grew heavy. "Yeah."

"You were a security specialist in the army, but never wanted to walk the beat?"

Even though the room was warm he felt a shiver move through him. Honestly, as much as he wanted to follow in his father's footsteps he knew he could never fill the man's shoes. "I thought about it."

She opened her mouth to say something else, but he pressed her hand to his lips. Wanting to redirect the conversation, because things were getting far too personal, he said, "We should get some sleep. You promised me a day of sight-seeing tomorrow."

She pulled the blankets up and covered them both, and he tucked her up against him.

"Tell me about the ring," she said quietly.

He exhaled slowly, thought about how tenacious she was being, and sighed with resignation. "What do you want to know?"

"Why is it so important?"

"My dad gave it to me."

She nodded. "I read the inscription. He's very proud of you. You two must have been very close."

He thought back to all the times he'd let his father down, and emotions hit like a nuclear blast, throwing him off balance. That's when he realized how much he missed the man. He missed him so goddamn much it hurt. He tried not to choke on his words when he said, "We weren't."

"Oh, I just thought..."

"I was a fuckup, Tallulah," he said before he could think

when she was a teen. It felt good to show him off, and charming man that he was, he seemed to win over the people who expected her to move home and marry Jason. She honestly hadn't anticipated that the townsfolk would fall for him, which when she really thought about it, put a crimp in her mission. When they called off this pretend engagement, the nice people that she'd known since she was a child were genuinely going to be disappointed.

They had dinner with her folks last night and the night before, and Garrett even suffered through a family game of Rummoli with her father and uncles while she fielded questions from her mother and aunts about her engagement and wedding plans.

Garrett seemed to fit right in, and when her father tested him on things such politics, religion and government, as well as a slew of other hot topics, Garrett rose to the challenge, impressing not only her father, but Tallulah as well. Still, she was pretty sure her folks would be happy when she called off the wedding, which made this farce a little bit easier on her.

As if feeling her gaze on him, he turned from the usher he'd been speaking with and glanced her way. They exchanged a long look, his eyes sweeping over her, and she bit back a small, knowing smile as her chest rose and fell with a deep intake of breath.

For a brief moment, she allowed her mind to drift, imagining that he was up there waiting for her. Instinctively, she placed her hand over her stomach, and wondered what it would be like if she were pregnant with his child.

Of course he'd been up front with her right from the start and warned that he wasn't father material, but her maternal instincts told her otherwise. Garrett Andersen would make an amazing father. She suspected he was the only one who didn't know it.

"You're flushed." Kat's gaze moved over Tallulah's features

as she pressed the back of her hand to Tallulah's forehead. "Are you sick?"

"It's warm in here."

"Are you sure you're not sick?" Kat continued to glare at her as organ music filled the church and the last of the guests arrived.

"Kat, I'm fine. Honest."

She sighed. "You're probably flushed from all that great sex you're having."

Once again Tallulah's thoughts returned to the deliciously naughty things they did with the scarf the other night and a shiver moved through her when she revisited the way he'd bound her, and pushed her past her comfort zone. She'd never been restrained before and it surprised her at how comfortable she felt with him doing it, how easy it was to be naked in front of him. But most of all how he'd given her total control of their sex play. As she told him what she wanted, what she needed, it felt like she'd bared more than just her body to him.

He encouraged her in ways no one ever had before, helping her discover things about herself, empowering her in ways she'd never imagined. It occurred to her that he was way better at reading her and more in tuned with her needs than anyone, her family included.

She couldn't deny that it felt so right to be held by him, and she'd found solace in his touch, his kisses, his lovemaking. The night on the elevator when they were discussing Ving and Jenny, he'd so much as told her he didn't care about her, and at the time she was glad of the reminder. What was between them was sex. Albeit great sex. But sex nonetheless.

But everything in what they did later that night, and every night after, the way he'd talked to her, touched her, made her tell him exactly what she wanted, felt like it was so much more than just casual sex. It felt like he'd taken her on a journey of self-discovery.

Why would he do that if he didn't care?

Then, when they'd engaged in pillow talk she realized there was so much more to this man than she knew. There were things he didn't want to tell her. What happened between him and his father? What happened in Afghanistan? What made him think he'd let everyone down?

"Ah, are you okay?" Kat asked.

"Yeah, why?"

"You have a strange look on your face."

"I'm okay."

Kat rocked back and forth on her too high heels, her upswept hair bobbing on her head. "Oh boy."

"What?"

"What's he done to you?"

Jenny came from the backroom looking like a real life princess and a hush fell over them all. Tallulah smiled and remained quiet until the beautiful bride took her place at the back of the line.

"What are you talking about?" Tallulah whispered, as Garrett came her way.

Kat pitched her voice low. "You look like a lovesick puppy."

"I do not," she said, leaning in so the others couldn't hear them.

A worried look came over her friend's face, and she grabbed Tallulah's hand. "Has he changed his stance on marriage and children?" Kat asked.

Tallulah gave a perplexed shake of her head. "No, why?" she asked as Garrett closed the distance. He cocked his head as he passed by her, and from the play of emotions on his face, she worried that he could see into her soul, see that she felt things she knew better than to feel.

Kat gave her hand a comforting squeeze. "Then you'd better pull yourself together, Lu. Otherwise you're going to end up in a world of hurt."

A nervous sensation settled in her gut as she thought more about their pillow talk. Garrett said he always let everyone down. She wasn't sure what had happened to make him feel that way, but knew his scars ran deep. She twisted the ring on her finger and wondered more about this security job he was after, and what the Committee knew that she didn't.

"I'm fine," she said, even though she wasn't so sure anymore. When they started this charade it never occurred to her that she could actually fall for him. She knew every-thing about him threatened her sexually, yet she never expected her emotions to get the better of her.

The music started, and Tallulah put her worries to the back of her mind as she walked slowly down the long aisle. As all eyes turned on her and she drew a calming breath as she stepped up to the altar, the other bridesmaids following along and taking their positions beside her.

When the bridal march started, she looked at Jenny on her brother's arm as he stepped into his father's role to walk her down the aisle. It occurred to her how well he filled those shoes, how he wasn't letting his sister down at all.

Before she knew it she was lost in Jenny and Ving's cere-mony. After the rings and kisses were exchanged, she followed the newlyweds out into the main foyer. They all formed a line and greeted guests before they made their way to the park for pictures.

With her feet killing her from standing in heels for so long, she was about to leave the church but then she felt Garrett behind her. She didn't have to turn to look. The scent of his skin, the warmth of his body as it reached out to her told her it was him long before he spoke.

"Hey," he murmured into her ear and a fine shiver tingled all the way to her toes. Everything from the sound of his voice behind her, his body pressing against hers in a familiar way, to the protective way he placed his hand on the back of her neck, did the weirdest things to her insides. It took all her effort to remind herself this thing between them wasn't real. "Everything okay?" he asked his breath hot on her nape.

She plastered on a smile, but feared her eyes would betray her emotions when she turned to him. "Yes, why?"

With his eyes fixed on her mouth, he curled a strand of her hair around his index finger and as heat and strength radiated from him, she reveled in the sensations her brought out in her. "You had a strange look on your face earlier."

"It's the wedding," she said. "They make me emotional."

He angled his head, his eyes piercing. "You sure that's all?"

She nodded, and taking her by complete surprise, his fingers splayed across her stomach in a soothing caress. "I thought you might have been having trouble."

Her heart galloped and emotions bombarded her. She braced herself, his compassion overwhelming her as longing swept through her. "I'm okay," she assured him as the church cleared. Feeling a bit panicky, she had to get out of there, needed to put some distance between them before she did something she might regret. Something like tell him she was imaging him as the father of her children and that's why she had the strange look on her face. "We should go."

She made a move to leave, but he cupped her elbow and hauled her against him. His big hands spanned her waist and his touch sent shivers skittering through her limbs.

His eyes darkened with desire, and his mouth settled firmly over hers. She sensed his possession, the hunger inside him and it gave her a rush. His hands slid over her skin, then he inched back, cupped her face and whispered, "You look beautiful." The heat and want in his voice made it difficult for her to get her next breath. Beneath the dress she could feel her nipples hardening and deep between her legs she moistened, her body preparing for so much more.

Someone cleared their throat and Garrett moved back, a sheepish look on his face.

Embarrassed, Tallulah quickly straightened her dress, squared her shoulders and turned to find her mother standing behind her. "I didn't see you there," Tallulah said and when Garrett grinned at her, she instantly realized that he'd seen her mother's approach. The kiss had been for show purposes, which once again reminded her that what was between them was a business arrangement.

"I guess we'll be making plans for you next?" Her mother's shrewd gaze went back and forth between the two.

"Soon enough," Tallulah hedged.

"When will you be ring shopping?" her mother queried, and even though her words were innocent, not meant to hurt, she could feel Garrett stiffening beside her.

"I love this ring," Tallulah said bluntly, and when Garrett's head jerked her way, like he was surprised by her sudden outburst, she squared her shoulders and in an even tone, added, "It's important to Garrett, which makes it important to me. I'd rather this on my finger than some showy diamond."

Her mother gave her an odd look, opened her mouth to say something then shut it again. "We'd better get going. We don't want to hold up the pictures."

Once she as out of earshot, Tallulah turned to Garrett and explained, "She's old-fashioned. She didn't know."

"She's right. You should have a proper ring."

Before she could say anything, he took her hand and they stepped out into the beautiful sunny afternoon. Fingers entwined, they made their way to the park across the street, and spent the next couple of hours posing for pictures.

Feeling a little faint in the hot sun, Tallulah found reprieve under a tall tree while the others mingled and fussed over the bride. She fanned her face, and watched from afar, and that's when she saw her mother talking to Garrett. The look on her mother's face was disconcerting, and one Tallulah had never seen before.

After a moment, Garrett looked past her mother's shoulders, and when he made eye contact with her, he made a move toward her. But her mother's arm on his stopped him mid-stride. They exchanged a few more words, then Garrett drove his hands in his pockets as her mother turned from him and cut across the wide expanse of manicured lawn.

"Everything okay?" Tallulah asked.

"I just wanted to thank Garrett."

Tallulah's head came back with a start. "Thank him? For what?"

Her mother was about to answer then concern moved over her face. She dropped down on the bench beside Tallulah and asked, "Is everything okay?"

"Too much sun," Tallulah said and fanned her face. "I'm feeling a bit faint."

"Garrett was about to check on you, but I asked if I could come instead."

She gave her mother an odd look and was about to ask what was up when her mother said, "Your father and I have been talking."

Tallulah stiffened, and toyed with the ring on her finger. "About?"

"Garrett."

Was her mother on to their charade?

"What about him?" she questioned nervously.

"He's a very nice boy. He seems to care for you a great deal."

Tallulah smiled and caught Garrett's glance, catching the

concern in his eyes. No words needed to be spoken for her to know what he was asking. She shook her head no and he nodded before stepping away. Even though he was ready to come to her rescue if she needed him, unlike everyone else, he never made her feel like a child, one who couldn't make her own decisions. Instead he made her feel important. Empowered.

"I'm glad you like him." Her stomach knotted, understanding how much this was going to complicate things when they finished their business transaction. Maybe she should just come clean and tell her mother the truth, let her know that she was a responsible adult and could make her own decisions. She opened her mouth but her mother cut her off.

"I've been watching you both and you seem different since the last time you were home."

"Different?"

"I'm not sure I can explain it. You just seem so happy, so in love." Her mother grabbed her hand. "I thought you'd be happy with Jason, living back here surrounded by those who care. But in the city you'll have Ving, Jenny and Garrett, and it comforts me to know you'll be surrounded by love."

Emotions welled up inside her, and she felt closer to her mom than she had in a long time.

"What can I say? I'm old-fashioned and just want what is best for my little girl. I thought I knew what was best for you, but well...maybe I don't."

She hugged her mother, exhaled slowly and began, "I'm not a little girl anymore though, Mom."

Her mother's blue eyes sparkled as she patted Tallulah's hand. "Oh, Tallulah, you'll always be my little girl," she said, laughing.

Tallulah caught Garrett's glance again, and when their eyes locked in a silent message the strength of their bond bolstered her confidence and gave her the courage she needed to finally speak her mind.

"Maybe so, but you have to understand I can make my own decisions. I, and only I, know what's best for me," she countered. "Even if things don't work out between Garrett and me, I still plan to live in the city. I love you and Dad and all you've done for me, but my life and work is in Austin now. It's where I need to be."

Her mother gave a slow nod. "You're probably right but someday when you have kids of your own, you'll see what it's like."

Tallulah thought about the doctor's prognosis and a lump lodged in her throat. She hadn't told her mother the bad news because the last thing she wanted to do was worry or upset her when she was dealing with Ving's wedding.

Her mother let loose a sigh, her glance perusing Tallulah's face. "I still don't like you living so far away, but something tells me, no matter what the future holds, you're going to be okay."

Tallulah squeezed her mother's hand, and deep in her heart she knew her mother would be disappointed when she broke it off with Garrett. But now that she opened her mouth and told her mother what she really wanted, her mother understood that Tallulah was going to make her own decisions, and was no longer going to do what was expected of her, which meant she wouldn't be pressuring her to come home. Tallulah smiled, surprised at how far they've both come in the last week.

After a long moment she asked, "Mom?"

"Yes."

"What were you thanking Garrett for?"

"Helping Mrs. Henderson."

"Mrs. Henderson?" she asked. "What are you talking about?"

"Garrett caught the Tanner boys causing mischief and put the fear of God in them. Those boys have been over there helping her every day since, and she's been baking up a storm for them." She paused and then said, "She thought Garrett was a fine young man and is telling anyone who will listen."

Tallulah arched a brow. "Really. And here I didn't think she liked anyone."

"I think it's because she's lonely. She lost her husband a few years back and her kids have moved away. I think she's secretly happy to be baking for someone again. I'd say Garrett must have picked up on that."

"He's very astute and very good with kids," she said.

"Especially delinquent ones," her mother said with a smile.

Tallulah nodded, and as she considered that longer, she wondered why he'd never followed in his father's footsteps. Just then she saw her own father walk by and her mother beamed at him when he cast a smile their way. Even after all these years it was clear how much they loved each other.

Tallulah turned to her mother. "Can I ask you something?"

"Sure. What is it?"

"How did you know Dad was the one?"

A distant look came over her mother's pretty face. "From the way he looked at me."

Tallulah nodded, because she'd seen that look. "How did he know you were the one?"

Her mother gave a small chuckle. "Don't worry, Tallulah. I see the way Garrett looks at you. You don't have anything to worry about."

With a heavy heart, Tallulah caught sight of Garrett in the crowd. She knew he was simply playing a role, but even if he wasn't—even if he really did look at her with love in his eyes

—what kind of future could they have anyway. They both wanted different things.

They continued to sit there in silence, more at ease with each other than they had been for a long time. By the time her stomach started grumbling, they were rushed off to the hotel banquet hall where they all took their seats. After the meal was served they were brought into a beautiful ballroom, and soon the lights were dimmed and the dancing began.

With Kat by her side, Tallulah glanced around in time to catch little Cassie dragging Garrett out onto the dance floor. It was a typical scene from any wedding, but the second she saw Garrett pick Cassie up and place her little feet on his her heart turned over in her chest. In that instant, she couldn't help but wonder what it would be like if they were a real family instead of a pretend one, but she knew better than to give her heart, or anything else, to a man who wasn't asking for it.

Kat snapped a picture of Garrett and Cassie, then the bright light flashed in Tallulah's eyes and momentarily blinded her.

She blinked. "Ah, a little warning might be nice next time."

"I wanted to catch you in the moment." Kat turned the camera back on the crowd, then nudged Tallulah when she spotted one of Ving's comrades at the bar. "What do you think of that badass?" she asked. Grinning, she added, "He looks like the kind of guy who'd be really good at bending a girl's will."

Tallulah laughed and was about to answer when someone came up behind her and said, "Would you like to dance?"

She turned and found herself face to face with Brad, or rather face to chest with him. She lifted her chin to meet his eyes. "I...uh..." she said.

A slow song came on and he held his hand out to her.

From the corner of her eye she could see Garrett glaring at them. The intensity in the way he stared at her made her breath catch, and her knees give a little.

"I guess I should get to know the woman who's stolen my best friend's heart, don't you think?"

———

With his mood blackening, Garrett swilled the rest of his beer and tried to ignore the possessive tug on his emotions as his best friend escorted Tallulah out onto the dance floor. He leaned against the bar, and was so busy trying not to care that he hadn't noticed Kat when she sidled up to him.

She finished the last of her drink. "Looks like I need another."

Thrumming his fingers on the bar top and trying to appear unaffected, he gestured the bartender for two more beers, but by God, it was frightening how jealous he felt, how much he wanted to go over there, punch Brad in the face and drag Tallulah back to their room where he could have her all to himself.

Kat snapped a picture of him, and he snarled at her. "What was that for?"

"You looked like you needed a little something to help you snap out of it," she explained then started taking pictures of Tallulah and Brad.

Garrett knocked back his beer, and tried for small talk. "So, you and Tallulah go way back, huh?"

"Yeah. Lu and I know everything about each other, every little secret," she said grinning.

She doesn't know every secret. Not like I do.

He watched her move on the dance floor, and it took all his effort not to stomp over there and peel Brad from her body.

Kat took a sip of her beer, then exhaled an exaggerated sigh. "At least I thought we did."

He turned to her. "What are you talking about?"

She had a worried, thoughtful look on her face. "I don't know. She's just...different somehow. I asked her about it, but she swears nothing has changed." She tapped her fingers on the beer bottle. "I think she's keeping something from me."

The song ended and Brad leaned in close to whisper something in her ear. Tallulah laughed, then headed off in the opposite direction. Garrett watched her until she disappeared into the hall. His jaw tightened. Where the hell she was going?

He was about to go after her, when Kat's words stilled him. "You know, I'd do anything for her."

"Does she need you to do something for her?" Garrett asked, staring out into the crowd. As he avoided her curious eyes, his body tensed because he suspected she was going somewhere with this.

"No." She touched his arm, forcing him to look at her. She narrowed her eyes, concern written all over her face. "She's just a nice girl, Garrett."

"I know that."

"A nice girl who needs a nice boy who wants the same things as she does."

His stomach clenched, and tightness settled deep in his chest. Okay, so he couldn't deny that Tallulah was easing herself right into his heart. "And this is your way of telling me to back off because I'm not that guy?"

She cocked her head and met his gaze unflinchingly. "I don't know. Are you?" she challenged.

He looked pointedly at Tallulah's best friend, and as he ran through the events of the last few days, he knew he was in a shit load of trouble. He never should have slept with her. He should have been stronger. She was a nice girl—sexy, sensitive, fun loving and compassionate—a girl who needed a man who could give her the things she wanted, a man who wouldn't let her down.

Fuck.

With that last thought in mind, he dropped his bottle onto the bar top, and pushed off the counter. "I gotta go," he mumbled and maneuvered his way through the crowd. He stepped into the well-lit hall, determined to take Kat's advice and end this dangerous game he was playing with Tallulah here and now.

Except that's when he saw her standing in the corridor outside the woman's washroom talking to her ex, Jason.

Every protective instinct he possessed came out full force as he clenched his fists and made a move toward her.

His footsteps gained her attention and she turned his way, but the confident, determined look on her face slowed him. He expected to see her shrink into herself, after all, she hated confrontation and didn't want to hurt anyone's feelings, even assholes like her ex, but when he saw her head held high, her back a little straighter, he stopped in his tracks.

She turned away from Garrett and that's when he realized she had the situation completely under control. He stood there listening to the tail end of their conversation, and while he noted the way she chose her words carefully, always sensitive to others—a quality he truly loved—she wasn't backing down in the face of pressure.

"I'm not a child, Jason," she continued while Garrett jammed his hands into his pockets, giving her the space she needed, even though he wanted to beat the living shit out of Jason, and take Tallulah into his arms. "I don't need anyone telling me what to do," she said, her voice steady, convincing.

"Lu," he murmured, "but we—"

Tallulah put her hand up, palm out to stop him. "I know what's best for me." She wagged her finger back and forth between them. "And I also know you don't want this any more than I do."

Guilt moved over his face and that's when Garrett got the impression that he was being pressured every bit as much as she was. Jason opened his mouth to say something, then clamped it shut.

"You should go find Kelly. You probably have some explaining to do."

He nodded and looked past her shoulder to make eye contact with Garrett, and if Garrett wasn't mistaken, from the way Jason was looking at him, he was trying to forge a truce between the two.

"You sure have changed," Jason murmured, then side-stepped Tallulah and disappeared into the lobby.

Garrett stepped up to her, and he couldn't help but feel proud. He ran his index finger over her bare arm and dipped his head, his eyes moving over her face.

"Are you okay?"

"Yeah," she said, and as his glance scanned her flushed features, he knew Kat was right. There was something different about her. He looked her over and couldn't help but compare the woman he'd met on the plane to the one who stood before him now. His mind flashed back to the sexy game he played with the scarf, to all the fun they'd had over the week, and on some level he hoped he'd played a part in her changes.

Garrett made a fist and nudged her chin in an attempt to lighten her mood. "I guess he was trying to mess with the wrong girl."

She laughed. "Turns out he's involved with Kelly Cameron, one of my old high school friends."

Garrett brushed a few wayward strands of hair from her shoulder. "Then why did he want to follow through with the pact he made with you?"

"I was the nice girl his parents wanted him to marry. They consider Kelly from the wrong side of the tracks. He'll have his work cut out for him."

"Folks around here sure do have a lot of pull."

"Small town," she said, like that explained everything.

"You never would have been happy with him."

"You're right." She smiled at him, and longingly touched her stomach. "If it wasn't for you I could very well be engaged."

"You are engaged." He grinned, and when he took her into his arms, everything inside him softened. "I must say, I like how you handled yourself."

Her laugh was edgy, churning with passion and color bloomed on her face when she leaned in and whispered, "I like the way *you* handle me."

A little shocked and a whole lot turned on by her boldness, he pulled back. Oh yeah, she definitely wasn't the same girl he'd met just a few days ago. As she looked at him with come-hither eyes, and his mind reflected on all the reasons he should stay away from her, his cock hardened. He fought an internal war, wrestling with himself as she stood there staring up at him, looking so goddamn beautiful and self-assured it took his breath away. He could feel his composure slipping, his resolve crumbling around the edges.

"Tallulah," he began, but then the next thing he knew she was in his arms. He wasn't sure who moved first, all he knew was that he needed to taste her, touch her, and lose himself in her for the rest of the night.

As he abandoned rational thought, they touched each other like their lives depended on it. His mouth smashed against hers and their tongues thrashed. Desperate for a deeper taste, he bit down on her lip. The kiss wasn't gentle, not by any means. It was hard, needy, demanding, and would undoubtedly leave her bruised tomorrow. He suddenly knew he was being rough because of his need to leave his mark on her.

"We should go," he said as their heated kisses left him yearning for so much more.

"Yeah, we should." Neither made a move. Instead they continued to touch and kiss, neither wanting to be the one to pull away first.

He threaded his fingers through her hair. "Tallulah, I'm serious," he said, her warm familiar scent curling around him as he reveled in the sweetness of her mouth. "If we don't move I just might take you right here in the hallway."

Desire flickered across her face and she gave him a devious smile, like the idea appealed to her.

"Oh, really?" His brow raised in challenge. "You want to go there with me?"

Her mouth twisted provocatively, and she gave a low, sexy laugh. "I suddenly find myself all about trying new things." Her warm breath wafted across his face, and his muscles bunched at the evocative thinning of her lips.

"Jesus, what have I done to you?" As a fever rose in him, he grabbed her hand, hurried into the lobby and ushered her onto the waiting elevator.

He pressed their floor and as the elevator started its ascent, she put her hands on his chest and ground her hot little pussy against his leg. Heat radiated from her sex and his balls tightened. Jesus H. Christ. Need whipped through his blood and his cock throbbed so hard in his unforgiving pants, it nearly shut down his brain.

He jabbed the stop button, knowing he'd never make it to the room. He also knew that even though he shouldn't be doing this, everything about her felt so goddamn right.

He backed her up and pressed her against the wall. He had to have her again, just one more time. Then tomorrow, after he returned to Austin, he'd get his shit together and carry on as normal.

He grabbed her hands and pinned them above her head, and she watched the action from the wall-to-wall, floor-to-ceiling mirrors. She sagged against him, her body soft, pliable beneath his hands. His mouth found hers again and she matched him kiss for kiss as he restrained her with one hand and touched her all over with the other, unable to get enough of her. He drove his knee between her legs, widening them as he pushed his thigh against her pussy. He rubbed her clit through her dress, moving his leg back and forth in much the same manner he would with his finger.

"Oh. God," she cried out. "You're going to make me—"

"That's the point, Peaches," he said, loving how he could do this to her.

Not wanting to bring her over just yet, he eased his knee out from between her legs. When she scowled, his hand stole up her dress and he cupped her sex. She moaned, and he felt her rush of breath on his neck as her wetness seeped through her panties.

"Are you hot for it, baby?" he asked, when he found her dripping with desire. "Are you hot for me?"

"I'm hot for you, Garrett," she answered breathlessly, and when she ran her pink tongue over her bottom lip, he tore her panties from her hips.

He swallowed her sexy gasp and pushed against her so hard he feared he'd break the mirror, but with basic need driving him, urging him to fuck her long and hard, there was nothing he could do to slow himself down.

"I'm going to fuck you, sweetheart. Right here," he said, impatience in his voice.

She moaned and gyrated against him, her body filled with such need his muscles began trembling. With shaky hands, he released his pants and freed his cock. Then he grabbed her and lifted her onto his hips.

Her eyes met his and his nostrils flared as the sweet peachy scent of her arousal filled the small space. He sucked in air and pulled her aromas into his lungs, letting it fuel his lust.

Desperate to be inside her he demanded, "Wrap your legs around me."

When she obliged he pushed her back against the wall, and positioned her until his cock was poised at her opening. He powered his hips upward as he lowered her onto him, driving himself into her so deep she let out a loud gasp and raked her hands through his hair.

"Garrett," she cried out as he stretched her. She began rocking, her body burning with need as he pumped into her.

His lips found hers and he kissed her hungrily as a tremor wracked his body. Primitive need raged inside him and through the thin material on her dress her nipples pressed against his chest, driving his passion to new heights. He increased the tempo, pumping so hard and so deep he feared he was chasing more than an orgasm.

He pounded into her, his groin smashing against hers as the crescendo of their union took him to the edge. She rocked against him, the sweet friction and the unbridled desire in her eyes, buckling his knees. He kept up the frantic rhythm until she threw her head back and cried out in bliss. Her hot juices dripped over his shaft and that's when he lost it.

"Oh fuck," he growled, the elevator swaying before his eyes as she bit into his shoulder. He took deep gulping breaths as he let himself tumble over the precipice.

He tensed, and his body stilled, reveling in the sensations as he spilled his seed into her. His climax sent ripples onward and upward through his body and somewhere in the back of his mind it occurred to him that he went at her like a rutting animal—an animal marking its territory. Panting, he held her tight and buried his face in her chest as he struggled to fill his lungs with air.

"So good," he murmured as her sigh of pleasure seeped under his skin. "So fucking good."

She squeezed her sex around him, milking him like she didn't want to miss a drop, and that's when it occurred to him that he'd been so crazed he'd forgotten to use a condom. Even though she was on the pill, and her chances of conceiving were slim, it wasn't like him to play with fate—twice.

The nervous sensation plaguing Tallulah all day had grown into a full-blown case of jitters as the dinner hour approached. It had been close to three weeks since she'd returned home from the wedding, saying a heartfelt goodbye to her family and friends. Her folks weren't happy to see her go, but were content to know that she was no longer alone in the big city.

If it wasn't for Garrett things could have gone down so differently for her. Honestly, she couldn't believe how fond her family had grown of him in only a few short days. Then again he was a very likeable guy and she hated that it was going to hurt everyone when she called to tell them the fake engagement was off.

She thought back to something Garrett had said to her, about her parents backing off and realizing she could make her own decisions when they saw her on the arm of the *right* man for her. She was well past the point of denying Garrett was that man.

She began pacing, and a shiver moved through her as she reminisced about the way he had taken her hard and fast in the elevator during the wedding reception. She'd never affected a man quite like that before—to the point of losing control—and thinking about how frantic and crazed she could make him, brought a smile to her face.

A noise sounded outside her condo. She pulled the curtains back and spotted Garrett parking his SUV. Wrestling her nerves back into submission, she walked to her door. Trying not to appear anxious, even though she'd been counting down the minutes until he came for her, she wrapped her hand around the knob and waited.

He knocked and she counted another second, then she pulled it open, not knowing how he'd receive her. They might be going to dinner together to impress the Committee, but right here, right now, they had no audience, no one to fool. Would he be all business, or would he want to pick up where they left off?

"Hi," she said sounding more breathless than she'd like.

He stood on her stoop staring at her longer than was comfortable, his gaze sweeping her black cocktail dress then back up to settle on her face. She fidgeted under his scrutiny, her hand going to her cheek. "Do I have something on my face?"

He laughed. "No, you look beautiful, Tallulah." He cupped her face in his hands. "I love it when you blush."

"I'm not blushing," she said.

His eyes narrowed, and he put his hand on her forehead. "No. Then you must be flushed. Are you feeling okay?"

"I'm okay." She was about to move, but his lips closed over hers, preventing her from checking herself in the mirror. The kiss was so passionate, so achingly tender it nearly stopped her heart.

He inched back and it took a moment for her to pull herself together. "What was that for?"

His grin weakened her knees. "I wanted to make sure we still had it."

"Still had what?"

"The role of the adoring couple nailed down." He looked past her shoulder, and a strange, melancholy look came over his face as he scanned her home.

"Did you want to come in?"

"I thought it might be good to look around your place before we go. Just to get a better insight in to your life in case there are questions."

She agreed and he closed the door behind him. He stepped farther into her condo, and as his presence overwhelmed the small space, she thought about how good he looked in his dark suit. How good he looked in her home.

"You've been working." His gaze honed in on the notes and papers strewn across her coffee table.

"I have my final interview tomorrow for the director's position. I want to be prepared."

The hard angles of his face softened. "You'll get it, Tallulah. I can feel it in my gut."

She nodded, then gave him a tour of her place. When they reached her bedroom, he stood outside the door and once again she caught that same strange look on his face.

"You have a nice home," he said, his voice dropping an octave.

"Where do you live, Garrett?" It occurred to her that they should visit his place before meeting with the Committee, so she could gain better insight into his life as well. Then again, he likely lived in a typical bachelor pad in the downtown core.

"Out in Jamieson Park."

Okay, that surprised her. "In suburbia?"

He shrugged. "When I was away I sent money home to help with things, but Mom banked it and she insisted I use it for a down payment on a house."

Grinning, Tallulah led him back down the hall to the front foyer. "Ah, I think it's her way of trying to tell you she wants grandkids."

"That will be up to Jenny and Ving," he said, looking a bit uncomfortable as he checked his watch. "We should go."

She grabbed her purse, and followed him outside. They made small talk as they made their way to the country club, where mingling and dinner would follow.

She thought about the role she'd be stepping into once again, and how surprisingly natural it felt to her now. Of course, Garrett was easy to be around, and played his part to perfection, which made it that much more effortless for her. Garrett suddenly swerved his vehicle to avoid a pothole and a wave of nausea gripped her stomach. She drew in a deep breath and slowly blew it back out. Sweat beaded on her upper lip. She pressed her finger there, and turned her face toward the window. Watching the scenery fly by as they made their way to the outskirts of town only added to the nausea.

"You okay?" he asked, breaking the quiet.

"My stomach is funny. I think I might be a bit nervous."

"You have nothing to worry about. They're going to love you. And once they see that I'm *stable*, settling down with a beautiful daycare teacher—soon to be director—I'll be a shoo-in for the job."

She was about to ask what was really behind the Committee's worries when he turned the SUV to the right and pulled into the parking lot of the country club.

He squeezed her hand. "There's one thing we need to do before we go."

"What's that?" He reached in to his glove box. "Oh," she said when he opened a velvet box to present her with a beautiful diamond.

"I picked it up today."

Her heart went in to her throat, and then she swallowed,

forgetting this wasn't real. "Garrett, it's...it's beautiful." She held her hand up, and wiggled the silver band on her ring finger. "But I really love this one," she explained, knowing his father's band held so much more meaning.

He pulled the silver band off her finger and replaced it with the diamond. "Yeah, but you should have a proper ring. Even your mother thought so."

"I did have a proper ring."

He went quiet for a moment, then said, "A stable guy gives his fiancée a proper engagement ring. If we're going to pull this off with this Committee, we have to pay attention to detail. It's what they'd expect from a guy trying to head up the new alarm response team."

"Right." She gave herself a quick lecture on what was real and what wasn't, as she held the ring out to look at it. "It really is beautiful."

"Okay, let's do this."

The short walk through the parking lot to the country club gave her time to gather her nerves. Garrett placed his big hand on the small of her back and guided her out back to the huge veranda overlooking the lake. All around her people mingled, and when a waiter came by with a glass of champagne she graciously accepted. Although after the first sip, her nausea returned tenfold.

"Garrett, my boy, there you are," a middle-aged man said and stuck his hand out for a hard shake.

"Dave, this is Tallulah Duncan, my fiancée. Tallulah, this is Dave MacLeod, my boss."

"It's nice to meet you, Dave." Tallulah offered him a warm smile as she fought back the queasiness clawing at her throat.

"Well, well, now what's this all about?" Dave asked, his curious gaze bobbing back and forth between the two of them. "When did you get engaged?"

Tallulah leaned in to Dave and in a conspiratorial voice

said, "You know Garrett, privacy is his number one concern and he's completely overprotective of me."

Dave nodded. "He does practice what he preaches."

"Which is why he's so good at his job," she added, falling into easy conversation with his boss. She held her hand out and displayed the huge rock as Garrett gave her a squeeze of approval. "He kept me all to himself until he put this big thing on my finger."

Dave laughed and she felt Garrett relax beside her. "Well I can't blame him for wanting to keep you all to himself. But now that you're here, come meet my wife and let's all get to know each other."

As Dave led her to a group of women, who were all chatting as they shaded themselves from the late afternoon sun, he cast her a curious glance and asked, "Tallulah, what do you do for a living?"

"I work at Stepping Stone Daycare."

"No kidding." A huge smile showcased the fine lines around his mouth. "My grandson goes there. It's a great place."

Her eyes widened as she put it together. "Trevor MacLeod?"

"Yes," he said beaming.

"He's a great kid." She grinned conspiratorially. "Lot's of energy."

Dave laughed. "That's a nice way of saying he's a little hellion."

Tallulah laughed. "Now, now, I would never use the word *little*."

He laughed harder and guided her to the group of women. "Nancy," he said, to a beautiful woman with a stylish silver bob and smiling blue eyes. "You're not going to believe this."

Before Tallulah knew it she was lost in conversation with Nancy, as well as the other wives of the Committee members.

Garrett dropped a kiss onto her mouth, and after a good show of possession, he stepped away and went off with the men to enjoyed scotch and cigars while they talked business.

Dinner was pleasant, if not a bit nerve wracking. Everything in the way Garrett kept casting her glances said he was hungry, but not for the gorgeous display of food before them. He charmed the men, while she charmed the ladies, bringing them to laughter as she recounted the story of how the two had met during her dance class.

She wasn't sure how she got caught up in it, but had agreed to go out sailing with the group next week, even if the thought of all those waves made her feel a bit ill. But if it would help Garrett secure the job, she'd take something for the motion sickness, climb on board, and do her best to enjoy it.

Night settled over the city blanketing it in black as a mosaic of stars lit up the skyline. Exhaustion pulled at her and she tried to stifle a yawn, but Garrett caught it and excused himself, letting everyone know Tallulah needed to be well rested if she wanted to keep up with his boss's grandson in the morning.

Once she was alone with Garrett in his vehicle, she exhaled, realizing how much she had actually enjoyed herself.

His hand slid across the seat and captured hers. His voice was low, soft when he said, "You were amazing tonight."

"So were you," she said, struggling to remember the big picture. They were just helping each other out, and enjoying the benefits in the process. "And I don't think you have anything to worry about. I know you'll get the job, Garrett. With or without me, you'll get it." She gave him a wink. "I can feel it in my gut."

Silence fell over them as he cast her a sidelong glance, then catching her by surprise, he quickly took a side road and spun the SUV in the opposite direction.

As they headed away from her condo, she glanced around and asked, "Where are we going?"

Heat moved into his eyes. "My place."

"Why?" she asked, sucking in a quick breath when she caught the ravenous way he was staring at her.

"Because it's closer than yours."

———

Garrett pulled into his driveway, and when they both climbed from his vehicle, he led her along the pathway.

"So this is where you live," she said, looking around at all the other houses on the block, her glance moving over the toys left on the lawns from the neighborhood children. "It's very homey."

He pushed the door open and ushered her in, but until he saw her standing in his entranceway, saw the way her mere presence warmed his house, he never realized just how empty and alone it felt. It made him realize how he'd barely furnished it. The entire bottom floor, a spot he'd planned to turn in to a man cave, still sat empty and unused.

Her eyes lit as she glanced around and as he watched her look at his sparse furnishings, his body grew needy for her again. She walked into his living room, and pulled his curtain to look out the back window, taking in his huge, fenced lawn —the only toy free lawn in the neighborhood—the grass dead from neglect.

"Your place is beautiful."

"You're beautiful," he corrected, capturing her hand to guide her to his bedroom, desperate to feel her in his arms again. The air around them charged as she looked around his room, taking everything in. Her smoldering eyes locked back on his. His mouth found hers, and he kissed her with everything he had in him, needing to touch, to feel connected on some deeper level.

"God, I've missed you so much," he whispered into her mouth as his hand went to the back of her dress. With one quick pull, he released her zipper and stood back to watch her little black dress fall from her body.

Color moved into her cheeks, and his cock grew another inch.

"Now you." She stood there in her bra and panties, her chest heaving slightly.

Garrett made quick work of his clothes, then reached behind her to release her bra before slipping a hand inside her panties. When he found her wet, he groaned in bliss.

She pushed against his chest. "I want to ride you."

He grinned, loving this bold side of her, the side that spoke her mind, took what she wanted.

"Do you now?"

She pushed him again, and his cock slapped his stomach as she guided him toward the bed.

"Sit on the edge," she said.

Garrett lowered himself onto the bed and watched as she hooked her fingers inside the waistband of her panties, and slid them down her legs. When she was fully naked he crooked his finger. "Come here."

She walked up to him, and he took one breast into his mouth as he brushed his thumb over her clit, preparing her for his girth. She wiggled against him and he inserted one finger, then another. Her muscles clenched around him, then he pulled his fingers and brought them to his mouth.

"I love the taste of you."

She came closer and wrapped her arms around him as she climbed over him. Jesus, she felt so good, so right in his arms. Her mouth was so hot against his skin as she buried her face in his neck, it filled him with a bone deep warmth.

Condom forgotten, she dropped down on to him, and just held him tight as they began moving, her body knowing his so well, knowing exactly what he needed. They were supposed to be having casual sex, but he knew there was nothing impersonal in the way they were touching, or the way her body was weaving some mysterious alchemy on his soul.

When she trembled, he slipped his arms around her and held her tight. Silence fell over them as they looked at each other, the emotions in her expressive eyes tugging on his own. He wanted to give her the world, anything, everything she's ever wanted. He took a breath and concentrated on the sensations she aroused in him. He knew he was in way over his head, that she had indeed taken him down a path he had no intentions of travelling.

She tumbled into orgasm, and his thoughts scattered as her muscles clenched around his cock. Her mouth found his, and when she kissed him deeply, he released high inside her.

They collapsed onto the mattress and dozed for a bit, waking throughout the night to make love again and again. When the sun crested the hills and she blinked her eyes open he dropped a soft kiss onto her forehead

"I missed this," he whispered.

She snuggled in closer. "You missed sleeping with me?"

He brushed her hair from her face, paying careful attention to the pounding of his heart and what it was trying to tell him when he said, "I missed waking up with you."

![10]

After taking Tallulah home early so she could get ready for work, Garrett drove to the office. He could barely concentrate on the new home security contracts he was trying to get wrapped up, not when his mind was too preoccupied with Tallulah, the things they did last night, and her job interview this morning.

The second lunch hour approached, he pushed his paperwork aside and walked out into the warm sunshine. The sun seemed to be shining a little brighter, and he noticed a new bounce in his step as he hopped into his truck and drove straight to her day care. He was eager to see how her interview had gone, but maybe he was just eager to see her again. He craved to sneak in one more kiss, one more touch, because last night wasn't enough to hold him over until the end of the week, when they planned a sailing excursion with the Committee.

He walked along the pathway, stepping on each cement frog leading the way to the front door. He stood outside for a moment and watched. When he caught sight of Tallulah, clapping and singing songs with a group of toddlers, his felt a tightness in his chest, right around the vicinity of his heart. As if sensing him there, she glanced up and the smile that came over her face when she saw him, brought light to his darkest corners.

She said something to one of the other teachers, who stepped in for her while she came to the door to meet him.

She pulled it open, smoothed her hair back, and smiled up at him. "Hey, what are you doing here?"

He exhaled slowly before saying, "I thought I'd take you to lunch, and see how the interview went."

Pleasure brightened her eyes. "Give me five minutes and I'll be right out."

Twenty minutes later he sat across from her at his favorite café and he thought about how beautiful she looked, and how easy she was to be with while they ordered soup, sandwiches and lemonade.

After the waitress left, he reached across the table to take her hands into his, needing the connection at all times. "So tell me. Did you knock them dead?"

She smiled and took a tiny pull of water from her straw, and if he wasn't mistaken she seemed to be having a hard time swallowing. "They loved my ideas."

"When will you find out?"

"Probably by the end of the week. How about you, have you heard anything more?"

He shook his head. "Are you still on for sailing at the end of the week?"

She pulled a face. "Yeah."

He arched a curious brow. "I take it you don't like sailing."

"I'm not a huge fan."

He shrugged. "We can bail."

She shook her head. "No, this is important to you,

Garrett. I'll take something for the motion sickness." He opened his mouth to protest, but she said, "I'll be fine."

His heart missed a beat. Jesus she really was the sweetest thing he'd ever met, and it was frightening how much he wanted her again.

"By the way." She wiggled her ring finger. "The staff at the daycare want to throw me an engagement party."

Before he could reply, the waitress came with their order, and as he dove into his sandwich, she nibbled on her whole wheat bread. That's when he took a good hard look at her, and noticed she seemed to be growing paler by the minute.

His eyes latched on hers, alarm registering inside him. "Are you okay?"

She shook her head. "I don't know. I'm feeling a bit...off."

He glanced at her stomach. "Is it...?"

She swayed in her chair, and Garrett jumped from his, catching her before she hit the table headfirst. "Okay, that's it. We're going straight to the clinic."

"I just need a minute." She held her head in her hands. "Then I'll be fine."

Ignoring her protest, he helped her to her feet, put his arm around her and practically carried her out the door. He shot the waitress a glance. "I'll take care of the bill later."

Less than five minutes later, after maneuvering through traffic and running every red light, they were at the clinic. She went through triage, and because her blood pressure was frighteningly low, they whisked her off to a treatment room, where, after learning of her medical condition, they proceeded to do a battery of tests, including an ultrasound of her abdomen and pelvis.

Garrett sat beside her bed, worrying about the results of her ultrasound. Had her medical condition worsened? Had he been too rough with her? Would they tell her she needed surgery sooner rather than later, and put an end to her dreams of ever having children of her own? Christ, he saw her with those kids today, and there was no one in the world more deserving of a family than her.

"How's the patient feeling now?" the young nurse named Jan asked when she came back into the room.

"Jan, how are you?" Tallulah asked, then turned to Garrett to explain. "Jan's daughter is in my ballet class."

"I'm good," Jan said, "And you seemed to be doing much better."

"I'm am." Tallulah forced a smile.

"Good. The doctor will be in to talk to you shortly." The nurse grabbed the blood pressure cuff and glanced at the water glass she'd filled earlier. "Make sure you get that in you. You won't be able to leave here until you get yourself hydrated."

Garrett gave her a puzzled look and thought about how she'd barely touched her lunch, how she seemed to have a hard time swallowing. "Haven't you been eating or drinking?"

The nurse secured the cuff on Tallulah's upper arm and smiled at Garrett. "Don't worry, Dad," she said. "It's normal in the first trimester. Most women can't keep anything down until they reach the fourteen-week period."

Dad?

Garrett's stomach punched into his throat and he stumbled from his chair, sending it flying backward. His gaze flew to Tallulah, who stared back at him with equal amounts of shock and excitement as that one word bounced around inside his brain and vacuumed the wind out of him. He gripped the side rail on her bed, and reminded himself how to breathe.

"What are you talking about?" His heart thumped wildly, praying he'd heard her wrong. He forced air into his lungs, but the examination room suddenly seemed too small, too suffocating. With the walls closing in on him he let go of the rail and stumbled backwards. He sucked in another sharp breath and shook his head. "This can't be. You must be mistaken."

"You mean you didn't know about the baby?" the nurse said, a nervous look on her face.

Baby?

"Tallulah," he said, shaking his head. "What's going on?"

She clutched her stomach, and a barrage of emotions moved over her face when she squeaked out, "I didn't know either."

The nurse inched back. "I...ah...I think I'd better go." She darted into the hall to leave them alone.

Barely able to focus his mind, he said, "I don't understand. How did this happen?" He gripped a fistful of hair, then tugged at his shirt collar as the news blindsided him. Feeling like he'd just been suckered punched, he blinked his eyes shut and murmured under his breath, "Jesus Christ, this can't be happening."

"Garrett, I didn't know," she said, panic edging her voice.

When he opened his eyes and saw the way she cradled her stomach, confusion and anger came at the same time. "You didn't know?" he asked, his tone taking on a hard edge. "How could you not know?"

She frowned. "How could I have known?"

"Maybe when you missed your period, it might have crossed your mind."

"I miss my periods all the time. I thought it was the endometriosis."

Ignoring her as his blood ran cold, and his thoughts scattered like the enemy in the line of fire, he shot back without thinking things through, "You wanted this, didn't you? You knew what you were doing all along. That first night when you seduced me, you had this planned, didn't you?"

She swallowed, and wounded eyes met his. Christ, he knew he was being a prick, a total fucking asshole, but he couldn't seem to help himself. Not when Tallulah was offering everything he wanted, everything he could never have.

"What are you talking about?" She tented her fingers in front of her face as water pooled in her eyes.

"You did this. You did this on purpose."

She shook her head hard, her hair flying around her shoulders. "Garrett—"

"You wanted this."

Her chin trembled slightly, but she lifted it high. "Is that what you think?"

"I told you I couldn't be a father."

"I never asked you to be." She glared at him for a moment. "Why don't you tell me what you're really afraid of, Garrett? What are you running away from? What happened with you and your father?" She gestured toward his scar, angry fire flashing in her eyes. "What happened in Afghanistan?"

His hand went to his face. "Do you really want to know?" he bit out.

"Yeah, I do."

"I fucked up, okay? I let everyone down. A family will never be the same because of me." He drove his fingers through his hair and exhaled sharply.

"How did you fuck up?"

Pain cut deep as he dredged up old memories. "I misread my comrade, and he opened fire on the innocent instead of the enemy. He took out a mother and father, then turned the gun on the kids."

Her eyes moved over his scar. "But you stopped him didn't you?"

He stilled. "How do you know that?"

"I saw the Bronze Star in your bedroom. You're a hero."

"I'm not a hero. I always let everyone down."

When he went quiet, she swiped at the water running down her face. "I'm sorry, Garrett, I know that couldn't have been easy on you, but you saved those two kids. You can't forget that."

"I orphaned them."

Sadness moved over her face. "Why do you think your father isn't proud of you?"

With his emotions in turmoil, old hurts and insecurities came rushing to the surface. Before he could think better of it, he blurted out, "I joined the army instead of the police force because I couldn't live up to his expectations. He was a great father, a great cop, great at everything. I couldn't compete with that. I could never walk in that man's shoes. So I thought somehow if I saved the world he'd be proud of me. But I couldn't save the world. Christ I could barely save myself."

"Garrett, I'm sure your father was proud of you."

"Yeah, well maybe you're right. What the hell do I know anyway? I clearly pegged you wrong. I never thought you were just another beautiful woman who played by her own rules and look how that turned out. Christ, maybe your family was right all along. Maybe you do need them to tell you what to do and show you what's best because clearly you can't make good choices on your own." He swallowed the bile punching into his throat and met her gaze. "Were you ever really on the pill?"

Her eyes flared hot. "You think I lied to you?"

"Did you?"

The anger on her face turned to hurt. "Is that what you think?"

"Yeah, that's what I think."

"Then you must be right. After all, you're the expert at reading people, right?"

"So you're admitting it then?" His head swam as another thought hit. He was good enough to impregnate her, but not good enough for anything else. But he didn't want anything else, right? Hell he had no idea what he wanted.

He glared at her and she pulled the blankets up to cover herself, before adding, "You know what, Garrett? Maybe the Committee is on to something." Her voice was even, controlled when she added, "Maybe you really are emotionally damaged."

Garrett scoffed. "Look at you. You finally found your voice, did you? Too bad you couldn't have learned to use it earlier and gone to battle with your family instead of hiding behind me. Then you wouldn't have needed a fake fiancé and we wouldn't be in this mess."

"If you didn't want me to speak my mind, maybe you shouldn't have taught me how."

"Tallulah—" he breathed out, his heart aching as he remembered that special night together. "You knew I didn't want kids, that they weren't part of our business arrangement. I told you I couldn't be a father."

Jesus Christ, all he ever wanted was to be a father.

"I never asked you for that."

"No, you just took it."

She angled her head away from him. "You should go."

He gripped his head and took deep breaths, his mind racing, trying to sort things through. God, how could he ever be a father and take care of something so tiny and precious when he couldn't even take care of himself.

"I want you to leave, Garrett."

"Tallulah, wait."

"No. Go, now."

He was about to protest, but what the fuck could he say.

Obeying her wishes, he turned toward the door but before he exited she said, "Just for the record, I'm not the one who gave up on you. You're the one who gave up on yourself. You would have been a great father and the only person who doesn't believe in you, is you."

 ●11

Tallulah woke up with a throbbing headache and a topsy-turvy stomach. She jumped from her bed and made a beeline to the bathroom where she spent the next twenty minutes throwing up. When she was finally able to stand, she glanced at herself in the mirror, but the swollen eyes staring back, the hair in total disarray, the pajamas that she'd been in for days was a reminder of the fight she'd had with Garrett. They'd both hurt each other, Tallulah wanting this baby and a life with Garrett every bit as much as he didn't want it.

She placed her hand over her stomach, and a mixture of joy and sadness rushed through her blood. God, she wanted a child more than anything in the world, and even though the life growing inside her was nothing short of a miracle, she wasn't the kind of girl who'd go against someone's wishes and take what she wanted.

With slow, careful movements, she padded softly to her kitchen, forcing herself to go to work after two days in bed. At least it was Thursday and she only had to suffer through today and tomorrow before the weekend. She glanced at her cell phone and noted all the messages from Kat. She'd been avoiding her best friend, not wanting to talk about the pregnancy, or that Garrett didn't want anything more to do with her...or their child.

She grabbed a few crackers from the cupboard and nibbled on them. When her stomach finally settled, she jumped in the shower. Once finished she put on her work wear, tried to hide her swollen eyes with makeup and left for the center.

The bright lights and all the smiling faces and hugs that greeted her helped cheer her up a little, but every now and then she glanced at the door, wishing she'd find Garrett on the other side.

It was a little before lunch when her boss called her into her upstairs office. Fighting another bout of nausea, she climbed the stairs and took a seat on the other side of Andrea's desk. That's when she noticed her application on the table and knew this meeting was about the position she wanted so badly.

"How are you feeling?" Andrea asked. "You're not still fighting the flu are you?"

"No, I'm feeling much better," Tallulah said, keeping her pregnancy to herself for the time being. "Thank you."

"Very well. I just wanted to let you know that the committee and I have gone over your application, and I'm afraid to inform you that we don't think you're suitable for the director's position."

The room swayed before Tallulah's eyes and she gripped the arms of her chair to keep herself balanced. "Not suitable?" she asked.

"That's right," she said and without even trying to soften the truth she explained, "This position requires someone who is assertive, someone who can speak their mind and persuade board members and the municipality to implement new rules.

Your ideas are brilliant, so we're going to hand them over to Janice."

"Janice? You're going to give the promotion...and my ideas to someone you hired three months ago?" She shook her head. "You've got to be kidding me?"

Tallulah climbed from her chair, and with her emotions and hormones all over the place, she said, "I've been working here for three years, giving this organization everything I have, writing reports and papers on how to better serve the children, and you're telling me I'm not suitable for the promotion?"

Her boss pushed back in her chair, and putting an end to the conversation she said, "I think the best thing for you is to go back to the classroom with the children."

"And what I think is best for me is to find an organization that values me and treats me with the respect I deserve." With that she scooped her reports off her boss's table and left the office. She gathered her belongings, gave a hug to all the kids she loved, and jumped in her car. Tears flowed fast and furious as she drove home, and she questioned the logic of her actions as she negotiated traffic. Now, not only was she pregnant and alone, she was also unemployed.

The second she entered her condo, she grabbed her laptop and booted it up. She pulled open her patio door and walked out into the sunshine, letting it warm her suddenly chilled body as she Skyped Kat.

Kat came on the screen. "Lu," she said, as soon as she saw the tears. "What's going on? I've been trying to get ahold of you for days. I even called Ving."

"You called Ving?"

"Yes, but he said he hadn't seen you either." Kat leaned closer to the screen, and Tallulah could see she was in her office at the hospital.

"Are you at home?" Kat asked and checked her watch. "What are you doing at home?"

"I quit my job today."

Kat gasped. "What happened?"

"I was the most qualified for the director's position, and they gave it to someone else."

"Shit," Kat said. "Why?"

"Because they said I wasn't assertive enough."

"Bastards. Hang on a sec." Kat turned to say something to a colleague, and Tallulah took that moment to think about things, like even though it stung, maybe her boss was right. Before she'd met Garrett she'd never do anything to rock the boat. If they needed someone to go head to head with the board, or government officials, she could see why they turned her down. Heck, last month she never even would have stood up to her boss, or told her what she really thought. She would have tucked tail and run.

Like Garrett is doing.

Kat came back on the screen. "But you know what, Lu, maybe this is the push you needed to start your own center. It's what you always wanted."

"Yeah, I thought about that, but I have something else to tell you." Tallulah thought about the miracle inside her and blurted out, "I'm pregnant."

Kat exhaled slowly and pressed her palm to her forehead. "Oh, my God, Tallulah." She went silent for a second then asked, "How did Garrett take the news?"

"How do you think?" Tallulah fought off a wave of nausea. "We're different people who want different things."

"Hey, I told you before, opposites attract."

"Sexually maybe."

"He's crazy about you, Lu. I could see it in his eyes at the wedding reception. You need to see those pictures yourself to understand. I'll get them scanned and forward them to you."

"I think what you saw was lust." She pinched the bridge of her nose, and sniffed. "We never should have pretended we were engaged, then none of this would have happened."

"Honey, I'm so sorry. I feel like this is my fault. I'm the one who talked you in to seducing him."

Tallulah shook her head. "No. You might have given me a little push, but it wasn't like I hadn't thought of it, or wanted to do it. I take full responsibility for my own actions."

"Do you think you should come home?"

"No. I just need to figure out what to do next."

Just then a noise at her gate gained her attention, and her heart jumped into her throat when she turned around to see her brother, Ving, standing there, his hands fisted, his body tensed for battle. That's when she realized he'd heard her entire conversation.

His nostrils flared and the muscles along his jaw clenched. "Where is he?"

———

Sitting at their favorite pub, Garrett took a long pull from his beer bottle and then slammed it down hard on the scarred and dented table. "Pregnant," he said. "How the fuck did that happen?"

Brad twirled his bottle. "You really want to know. Okay then, when a man is attracted to a woman..."

"Fuck off." Garrett ran his hands through his hair. "What I know is she got me so goddamn hot for her I forgot to use a condom. Twice at the wedding and again the other night."

"Hey, it takes two, pal. The blame isn't entirely hers."

Christ he hated when his friend was right, and after spending days rehashing their hospital conversation, he knew Tallulah didn't deserve what he'd said to her. "I told her up front I didn't want to have a kid."

"Did you ever think that on some level you forgot protection on purpose because you wanted to give her the baby, the family, she wanted?"

Garrett snorted. "What kind of psycho bullshit are you trying to sell me? You know I'm not cut out to be a father."

"Why?" Brad pushed.

"You know why."

"What I know, Garrett, is war is pretty fucking horrific and you couldn't have stopped or changed what happened over there any more than any of us could. It wasn't your fault your guy lost his shit, and you did the best you could in a bad situation. So don't you think it's time you stopped blaming yourself. Because if you don't, pal, you're going to lose the best thing that has ever happened to you."

Garrett's head came up with a start. "You mean Tallulah?"

"Of course I mean Tallulah." He took a swig from his beer and shook his head. "Jesus, you're denser than I thought. Come on, I see the way you look at her. You're crazy about her."

Garrett swallowed and thought more about Tallulah. Jesus, he never meant to hurt her. Deep in his heart he knew she was kind and sweet and had never manipulated him. He'd shot back at her and said hurtful things in anger—in fear. Christ, she wasn't the one with the problem. He was.

"You couldn't change the outcome overseas, but you can change the outcome here," Brad continued. "You're a guy who goes to battle for what he believes in, and yet when it comes to Tallulah you're so scared shitless, you've been fighting what you really feel and have been running in the opposite direction. Grow a set why don't ya?"

"Fuck, Brad, why don't you tell me what you really think," Garrett grunted.

"Okay, how about this then. If you're running away from Tallulah and the baby because you're afraid of letting them down, well guess what, pal, you've already succeeded in doing just that."

Sometimes he really hated how well Brad knew him.

Garrett pushed back from the table, and was about to get up when Ving came crashing through the door.

Shit.

"You son of a bitch." He stormed across the room. "You fuck with my sister, get her pregnant, and then walk away. What kind of a fucking guy are you anyway?"

"A pretty fucked-up one," Garrett said.

Ving leveled him with a glare. "Oh yeah, well you ain't seen fucked up yet."

Brad pushed to his feet but Ving ignored him, and before Garrett could even put his hand up, he took a hard hit to the jaw that sent him flying backward. He toppled over a table and crashed to the floor. Ving went after him, but Brad stepped between the two. Garrett climbed to his feet, wishing Brad would back the fuck off because he knew whatever Ving was about to dish out, he more than deserved.

Brad said something to Ving, which seemed to calm him down. Then Ving pointed a finger at Garrett and said, "You need to do right by her."

12

Night fell over the city as Garrett drove through the streets, sick at the way things had turned out with Tallulah and still unable to comprehend the idea that he was going to be a father.

A father.

He and Tallulah, along with Phillip McNeil—the other man vying for the lead security job—and Phillip's wife, were supposed to meet with the Committee on board the sail boat in less than twenty minutes. But the last thing he felt like doing was putting on a show, and pretending he was something he wasn't.

Yeah, okay, so maybe he *was* emotionally damaged. Hell, maybe he really didn't want this fucking job anyway. Honestly, when it came right down to it, by all rights Phillip should get it. He cared more about the position than Garrett ever did anyway.

He turned in to the marina and could already see a crowd on his boss's boat. He fixed his tie, and ran his hands through his hair, working to come up with an excuse for Tallulah's absence. Deciding to get this over with, he climbed from the vehicle, tried to wipe the snarl from his face as he walked along the aluminum gangway.

When he reached the yacht and heard familiar laughter, his heart lodged in his throat. Jesus Christ, he couldn't believe she was actually here, that after all the hurtful things he said to her, she'd still do this for him. He must have done something right in another life, because he sure as hell hadn't done anything in this one to deserve Tallulah.

His heart pounded harder as he stepped onto the boat and if sensing him there, Tallulah turned. Her eyes were bright with laughter, but the sadness lingering beneath the façade hit like a physical blow to the gut.

"There you are," she said, nursing a glass of water while everyone else drank champagne. "I told Dave you'd be running late." She grinned and wagged her finger. "That's my workaholic fiancé. Always working to the bitter end to make sure every job is done right." She went up on her toes and when he dropped a kiss onto her mouth he felt her body tighten.

He could hardly believe she was here, bragging him up in front of the others, following through with the charade and making sure he landed the job. The boat started moving, and when Dave placed a hand on Garrett's shoulder, urging him toward the stern where the other men were talking business, he watched Tallulah's face pale, her hand gripping the metal rail hard enough to turn her knuckles white. That's when he realized she never would have taken anything for the motion sickness, not when it could harm the baby.

He couldn't let her do this. Not for him.

"Wait," Garrett said. "We need to go back."

Her hair flared around her shoulders as she spun toward him. "Garrett, it's fine," she assured him, her voice full of panic as her eyes widened in warning.

"No, it's not fine. Tallulah's pregnant and she hasn't been feeling well. Sailing is only going to worsen her condition."

A chorus of agreement sounded and Dave made a circle gesture with his hand. Seconds later, the boat was back at the dock. Tallulah apologized, but the women fawned over her, giving her advice as Garrett guided her off. The all agreed to go to the country club in lieu of sailing, but Garrett politely declined, saying Tallulah needed her rest, and she didn't argue the point.

They stood on the marina face to face and once the sailboat was out of earshot, he put his hands on her arms and dipped his head until their eyes met. "You didn't have to do this. Not for me."

"We had a business deal, and I want to follow through." Her eyes moved to the welt on the side of his face, compliments of her big brother. "I heard what Ving did. I'm sorry."

"Don't be. I'm the one who's sorry. I never should have said... I'm such an asshole. None of this is your fault and you didn't deserve to be attacked." As she stood there staring up at him, her big eyes wide while he begged for forgiveness, he continued, "I just...when the nurse said I was going to be a father...I didn't know...I can't..." He breathed deep and his chest shook as he let it out. "I never meant to hurt you."

"I know," she said quietly.

"I told you I was a fuckup." He rubbed his scar. "I guess the Committee really was on to something."

Instead of agreeing or disagreeing, she looked out over the water. "I hope I didn't screw this up for you. Phillip is probably charming them right now."

"It doesn't matter. I don't even want this job anyway."

Her eyes moved back to his, and tension hung heavy. "No? Then what do you want, Garrett?"

He swallowed, hard, as conflicting emotions pulled his

thoughts in a million different directions. "I want to do right by you. I'll marry you."

Sadness moved over her face and when her hands closed over her stomach, his protective instincts flared. "No. I never asked you to marry me just because I was pregnant. I'm more than capable of raising a baby by myself if you're not interested in being a part of our lives. But if you want to be a part of my life, and our baby's, I don't want it to be because Ving told you to or because you think it's the honorable thing to do. I want you to do it because you want to." Her voice dropped, and became strangely quiet when she added, "Because you want *us*."

His chest squeezed. "Tallulah," he said, scrubbing his hands through his hair and trying to figure out how to make this right with her.

"I have to go." With that she walked to her car, climbed in and disappeared into the night.

As he watched her go, he thought about his conversation with Brad. She was the best thing that had ever happened to him and he was nothing but a goddamn chicken shit. But what if he went after her, begged her to marry him, and then only ended up letting her down. Letting their child down.

You already did.

He trudged back to his truck, drove around for endless hours, trying to sort out everything that had happened over the last month. Knowing he needed to talk to Tallulah before his head exploded, he headed to her place. Panic invaded his gut when he saw her car wasn't there. He grabbed his cell and punched in her number, but when she didn't answer, he headed to Ving and Jenny's on the other side of town. He pulled into his brother-in-law's driveway, and saw Tallulah's car. But Ving's truck was gone. With unease moving through him, he rushed up the steps and pounded on the door. When he got no answer, he called his sister's phone.

"Garrett," she said quietly. "Where are you?"

Fear moved down his spine. "At your place."

"I was just about to call you."

"Where is she?" he asked, running back to his vehicle because he feared he already knew the answer.

"At the hospital. She had some bleeding and called Ving."

Goddammit she should have called me.

"Is she okay?"

"They gave her something to help her sleep. She hasn't been getting much of that lately."

He threw the SUV into gear and whipped out of the driveway. "And the baby?"

"The baby is fine."

"I'm on my way."

Garrett sped like a madman through the streets and when he reached the downtown core, he had no idea how he'd managed to make it to the hospital without a ticket. He hurried inside and stopped at the desk to ask for her room number.

"Only immediate family," the nurse said.

"I'm her fiancé," he explained and as soon as the nurse pointed out where she was he bolted down the corridor. When he reached her room and saw her sleeping, Jenny and Ving sitting next to her, it felt like his world had been ripped out from underneath him.

He stepped up to Tallulah, and worked to breathe as he brushed his thumb over her cheek. Then he glanced at his sister. "Jenny," he croaked out.

Jenny climbed to her feet and hugged him. "She's going to be fine, Garrett."

"The baby?" he asked again.

"They did an ultrasound and the fetus is firmly seated." A noise crawled out of Garrett's throat a half sob, half cry of relief. "The doctor said the bleeding wasn't serious, but since she has severe endometriosis, she's going to need special care during her pregnancy."

"I'll take care of her."

"Because you've been doing such a fine fucking job of that already," Ving said, pushing past him.

"Jesus, Jenny," he whispered, his throat too tight to swallow as Ving disappeared into the hall. "What the hell have I done?"

"Don't worry about him. He'll be okay once you do the right thing." She paused and said, "You are going to do the right thing, right?"

"I tried. I told her I'd marry her."

"You told her you'd marry her? God, sometimes you can be so dense." Jenny shook her head. "Do you really think that's what she wanted to hear from you?"

"I...I..." Christ, he was such a fuckup. He closed his eyes in distress.

"You should probably also know she didn't get the director's position and quit her job. So she has a lot of stress on her right now, which is probably what brought this on."

His lids flew open, and everything inside him twisted into knots, his heart so heavy it became difficult to stand. "She quit?"

"Yeah, she basically told them where they could go."

"She did?" He fisted his hair and looked at her sleeping so quietly on the bed, the IV in her arm replenishing her fluids. "She never told me." Jesus, she was so strong, courageous and brave. Even without a job she was determined to stay here, face her responsibilities and raise her family, with or without him, when she could so easily have tucked tail and run back to her folks and let everyone else take care of her. He was the one who was chicken shit. Christ, maybe he could learn a thing or two from her.

He cleared his dry throat, rattled by the emotions she

brought out in him. He scrubbed his chin with his palm, and when a noise in the hall pulled his attention, he glanced over his shoulder, then back at Jenny.

"I called Mom." He gave Jenny a curious glance. "It's her first grandchild," she explained.

"What does she know?"

"Everything."

Fuck.

Garrett dropped down into the chair next to Tallulah's bed, and Jenny stepped into the hall. A few minutes later his mother and Donovan came in to sit next to him.

His mother wrapped her arms around him and it took every ounce of strength he possessed not to break down and sob like a goddamn baby.

"So you're going to be a dad," she said quietly.

"Looks that way."

His mom held Donovan's hand and looked heavenward. "Your father would have been so proud. I know he can't be here, but I bet he's looking down on you with a huge smile on his face."

A strange strangled noise lodged in his throat and he propped his elbows on his knees and rested his forehead in his hands. "I somehow doubt that," came his muffled reply.

"What are you talking about?" Donovan piped in.

Emotionally battered, Garrett rubbed the band on his pinky finger, then scratched at the scar on his face, and that's when he noticed Tallulah still had the engagement ring on. "I never gave him anything to be proud of," Garrett said.

"Garrett, there was no man on the force more proud of his son."

His head came up with a start. "What are you talking about?"

"He talked about you all the time." Donovan rolled his eyes before saying, "To anyone who would listen. I mean, I loved you like you were my own kid, but enough already," he said laughing.

Garrett shook his head, hardly able to believe what Donovan was saying was true. "I doubt that."

"If you don't believe me, head on down to the precinct. Everyone knew your every milestone. From your first tooth, until you joined the army. That man was damn proud."

"But I never did anything he wanted."

"Didn't mean he wasn't proud."

A long pause, and then, "But I could never have lived up to his expectations of me."

Donovan eyed him, his look thoughtful. "Why is that, Garrett?"

"That man did everything right. I couldn't compete."

"Did you somehow think you were in competition with him?"

"No...yes...I don't know. I guess I just never thought I could follow in his footsteps because nothing ever scared him."

Donovan let loose a harsh bark of laughter. "Believe me, we all have our issues, but as adults we're just better at dealing with them. Or hiding them," he said solemnly. He glanced heavenward. "He was a courageous man on the streets. I'll give you that. But he certainly wasn't fearless."

Garrett scrubbed his hand over his chin. "He wasn't?"

"I spent a lot of hours with that man and let me tell you, he was scared of one thing and one thing only."

Finding it hard to believe that his father was afraid of anything Garrett raised a skeptical brow and asked, "What was that?"

"Raising you and your sister. Your father would rather face the streets any day. Isn't that right, Diane?"

When his mother nodded and patted Garrett on the knee, Donovan continued, "He said the streets weren't nearly as scary as rising kids. He was always afraid of messing it up and doing something wrong by you two. But you know what, Garrett? He did it anyway. He faced his fears and did it anyway." Donovan gave a slow nod. "And when I look at you and your sister, and see what fine, upstanding adults you've both become, I know he did a damn great job."

Garrett swallowed, sorting through everything Donovan had just told him. With his heart pounding so hard he was sure his mother and Donovan could hear it, he shifted to face his mother.

"I'm sorry," he said quietly.

"Garrett, you have nothing to apologize to me for."

His throat was so swollen he could barely speak. "Yeah, I do. I took off after Dad died. I left when you and Jenny needed me."

"Garrett, we all grieve differently, and I knew that's what you were doing. Besides, we did okay, and we all got through this in our own way."

"But Jenny, she went through that rebellious stage. I should have been here."

She wagged her finger at him. "Jenny is my responsibility not yours, and just look at her today. I must say I did a fine job with her." She held his hand and squeezed. "Just like I did a fine job with you. I'm so proud of you two."

"Your mother is a strong woman," Donovan said.

"And I raised a strong son," she replied, smiling at Garrett before she turned her attention to Tallulah. "I think you two need some time alone." She climbed to her feet, and pressed a kiss to his forehead. As he watched his mother and Donovan leave, Garrett fought back tears.

A new sense of calmness came over him as he stood and walked to the bed, the knot in his stomach loosening. He took Tallulah's hand in his and cursed himself for being so cruel to her. She was sweet and kind, so easy to love, and so easy to be with that he could feel her affection even when she was asleep.

He thought more about Tallulah and how she always had faith in him, even when he didn't deserve it. She never stopped believing in him even when he didn't believe in himself. He'd told her to battle for what she wanted, and yet fear made him run away from everything he'd ever wanted, everything Tallulah was offering.

Christ, if his father could face his fears, then he could damn well do it too. And maybe, just maybe, it was time to join the force here in the city, and instead of trying to fill his father's shoes, just walk quietly and proudly beside them.

Just then Jenny came back in. "The nurse said she's going to sleep through and we should all head home and do the same."

Garrett shook his head, a wave of possessiveness swamping him, because he knew deep in his heart he and Tallulah belonged together. He'd pushed her away because he was scared of the things she made him feel, the things she made him want, but he was tired of being afraid.

"I'm not leaving."

As he stared at the beautiful woman he wanted in his life, he knew he wanted to become the guy she needed him to be. Christ knows she made him care, and gave him the courage to want to try. He felt a rush of love and stood there a moment longer, thinking about everything that had happened over the past few years, and knowing it was time for changes, time to let go of the past and concentrate on the future. But they couldn't have a future until they started at the beginning. And he knew just what he had to do.

Sucking in a long, breath as he warmed to the idea and let the decision settle into his brain, he turned to Jenny. "I need a favor."

13

Tallulah woke up feeling completely refreshed and pain free. She glanced around to gather her bearings, then stretched out her limbs. Feeling more rested than she had in a long time, she spotted Garrett asleep in the chair beside her and her heart tightened inside her chest. Fighting down the barrage of emotions, she turned to the nurse and watched her take her vitals.

"The baby?" she asked nervously, even though they'd told her last night everything looked good.

She smiled. "Still perfectly fine." Tallulah relaxed and the nurse nodded toward Garrett. "Should I wake him?"

Her heart jumped again when she turned Garrett's way and she worked to sound casual when she said, "No, he looks so peaceful, we should let him sleep." After the nurse took her blood pressure, which fortunately had stabilized, the doctor walked in.

"Am I free to go?" she asked.

He flipped through the pages on his clipboard and read a few notes. "Yes. But you have to take it easy for the next few days. No stress. You're high risk, and you need lots of rest and relaxation."

She nodded in agreement, then spent the next few minutes speaking with the doctor while her IV was removed. When they left the room to give her privacy to dress, she pulled on her clothes and felt a little rush of love as she gave Garrett one last look. She'd thought about waking him, talking to him. But what was left to say?

With a heavy heart she left the hospital, called a cab and went to Ving's to pick up her car. From there she drove through the quiet Saturday morning streets to her home. She plopped herself down on her sofa and stared at the television set, but her mind was so preoccupied with Garrett, the baby, her job—or lack thereof—she needed to find something else to occupy her mind and ease her stress.

Deciding to head to the health club to oversee her morning ballet class from a comfy chair, she threw on her gear, jumped in her car and headed across town.

"Good morning," she greeted the girl at the counter, then slipped inside the small classroom reserved for her, to find a few of her students already there. She grabbed a chair and rifled through her bag for her music.

"You know you should be home resting, right?"

She glanced up to see Nurse Jan as her little girl joined the others for warm up. Tallulah patted the chair. "If I'm not sitting here, I'll just be sitting at home. Are you just getting off work?" Tallulah asked.

Jan stifled a yawn and nodded. "I'm heading home to sleep. Jacinda's dad will be here for pick-up time." She waved to her daughter. "I'd better get going, but you make sure you take care of yourself."

"Don't worry. I'm taking it easy and would never do anything to harm the baby. And I didn't want to let the kids down." Not to mention that she needed something to occupy her mind.

She gave Tallulah a hesitant look. "Your fiancé stayed there the whole night with you."

She nodded. "He was still asleep in the chair when I woke."

"He was pretty worried about you and the baby." Tallulah went quiet and Jan went on to explain, "He told me if you needed blood, he was a universal donor."

"He did?"

"Yeah, he said he had a spare kidney too." She chuckled. "I know it's not funny, and I shouldn't be laughing…"

Tallulah grinned. "Really, he said that?"

"He offered every spare organ he had, but I think he would have given you his heart if you needed it."

Tallulah swallowed, realizing his heart was the only thing he wasn't offering her. She thought of his marriage offer, something he felt he needed to do out of duty, but she didn't want to be his wife if his heart didn't come with the proposal.

With that Jan left and Tallulah's phone beeped. She pulled it from her bag, and clicked on the messages from Kat. "*This was when he was watching you dance with Brad,*" the message said, and when she saw the pictures, saw the look on Garrett's face, her world tilted upside down. Tears pooled in her eyes, and her stomach knotted because she recognized that look, had seen her father give it to her mother millions of times.

She touched the screen and looked deeper into Garrett's eyes. She saw love shining there, but just beneath the surface she saw something else—something that resembled fear. She thought about all the things he'd said to her, about his father, his time overseas, how he always lets everyone down, and that's when a new calmness came over her. Maybe they weren't so different after all. When it came to people they cared about, they both retreated into themselves for fear of hurting someone they loved. But Garrett had taught her to stand up for herself and fight for what she wanted. Tallulah believed in Garrett, even when he didn't believe in himself, so was she really going to sit there and not fight for what she wanted, what she knew he wanted?

Deep in her heart she knew he loved kids, knew he was lost and searching for a way, and dammit, she was just the girl to help him find it.

With her heart racing, trying to figure out her next step, she put on the music, and gave instructions from her chair. But when the tiny hairs on her arms lifted, she didn't need to look up to know Garrett was standing there. She felt his presence long before she saw him and didn't miss the giggles coming from the girls.

"Tallulah," he whispered, an urgency in his voice, one she'd never heard before. Her breath hitched when she lifted her head saw him standing there in a pink tutu. As she stared at him, she didn't know whether to laugh or cry.

"What are you doing?" she asked, shaking her head, loving this crazy, playful side of him. "Where did you ever get that?"

"Jenny's." He looked down sheepishly, his tension visible. "We had to stitch a few together."

"Well you look ridiculous."

And adorable.

He arched a challenging brow. "But it will make for a good story, right?" When she offered him a warm smile, and he returned it, she knew in an instant that he was going to be okay, that everything was going to be okay. He held a shaky hand out to her. "I think we should start again. I'm Garrett. Garrett Anderson."

"Lu," she said, grinning. "But you can call me Tallulah Duncan."

A moment later the smile fell from his face, then he

grabbed both her hands and lifted her from the chair. "Tallulah, I'm sorry. I'm sorry about everything."

Her throat closed over, making speech difficult. "Garrett," she managed to get out, but he pressed his finger to her lips.

"You make me care," he said. "You make me want to try. I want to do right by you and the baby."

"I want you to be doing it for the right reasons."

His face softened and he smoothed her hair back. "Don't you see, Tallulah, I'm in love with you and want to be the man you need."

Tears filled her eyes. "You are that man, Garrett." Her heart swelled inside her chest as she poked him in his. "You're the only one who doesn't know it." When she saw the way he looked at her, the same way he looked at her in the picture Kat had sent, the tears fell harder, because in that instant she knew he was giving her every bit of himself, even his heart. "I know you're frightened. I'm frightened too," she said. "We might not always do what's right, and we'll make mistakes along the way, but know that you'll always be my hero." She took his hand and placed it on her stomach. "*Our* hero."

He looked deep into her eyes. "Thank you for always believing in me, and giving me everything I've ever wanted."

She swallowed the lump in her throat. "Thank you for helping me with my folks, my ex, and showing me how to battle for what I wanted. If it wasn't for you, I could very well be engaged."

He removed the diamond from her finger, then slipped the silver band off his pinky to place it back on her ring finger, where it always belonged. "I told you this once before and I'm telling you it again, you *are* engaged."

"Garrett," she choked out, her heart overflowing with the love she felt for him. Then she let her hands drop to her sides and with a chilling tone, she said, "You once told me I should never marry a man I didn't love."

His mouth dropped open and his body stiffened. "Oh, I..." He scrubbed his hand through his hair and spoke in whispered words. "I thought..."

"So the answer is yes." She laughed and slid her arms around his waist and when he realized she was teasing him, he let loose an agonized breath. She gave him a playful wink. "Maybe I owed you that."

"And I believe you're going to pay for that," he teased in return, then his eyes turned serious. "I love you, Tallulah."

"I love you too."

"I think I loved you from the first second I saw you in my seat. I never thought I believed in love at first sight or whirlwind relationship, but you changed all that for me. You changed everything for me." His warm glance moved over her face and his heat reached out to her, warming her soul. "I want to have a family with you, I want you to help me make my house a home, and fill it with a ton kids."

She pulled a face. "Ah, a ton? This one was a miracle..." Her words died away, thinking about how happy she was to have a baby, Garrett's baby.

He laughed, a glint of humor in his eyes as he enclosed her in his arms. "No Tallulah, I want you to fill it with other peoples' kids." When she gave him a perplexed frown his glance dropped to her mouth and he explained, "I want you to open your own daycare. I want you to turn the empty lower level of my—our—bungalow, and the outdoor space into the dream center you always wanted."

Everything inside her trembled with the love she felt for him, and her breath caught in her throat. "You do?" she managed around a tongue gone thick.

His lips closed over hers and when he kissed her with emotion and tenderness, she could feel the weight of the world drain from his shoulders, and knew his scars were healing. As deep contentment settled into her bones, all the little girls in the class started giggling, reminding them that they had an audience. He pulled back and the grin he gave her was so adorable, it weakened her knees. "I hope we're having a boy," he whispered and ripped the pink tutu from his hips. "Because I never, ever want to wear one of these again."

"But you would if you had to right? If your little girl asked you to?"

His lips twitched in amusement and proving once again that he was the man she always knew he was, that he was most definitely a real life hero, he said, "Yeah, of course I would."

AFTERWORD

Thank you so much for reading, HIS TROUBLE IN TALLULAH, in my Line of Duty series. I hope you enjoyed the story! Be sure to check out the other 6 books in the series. Please keep reading for an excerpt of HIS TASTE OF TEMPTATION.

- His Obsession Next Door
- His Strings to Pull
- His Trouble in Tallulah
- His Taste of Temptation
- His Moment to Steal
- His Best Friend's Girl
- His Reason to Stay

Interested in leaving a review? Please do! Reviews help readers connect with books that work for them. I appreciate all reviews, whether positive or negative.

Happy Reading,
  Cathryn

HIS TASTE OF TEMPTATION

Just when she thought her morning couldn't get any worse.

Madison Graham let out a sputtering yelp. Unfortunately, with a stuffed-up nose and well on her way to a major case of laryngitis, it came out sounding more like a Pekinese dog's yappy bark rather than the desperate cry of a woman in need of help.

"What the hell," a sleepy voice grumbled from behind her. "Ah, shit. Not again."

With her hand inside the hole in the wall that had yet to be fixed since their last plumbing disaster, Madison cupped her palm over the end of the broken pipe, struggling to stem the water flow before it did any more damage to her bathroom, or worse, leak through to her bakery on the ground floor below. Shooting a frantic glance over her shoulder, she saw Jonah Crosby, her childhood best friend and current roommate, and gave an aggravated shake of her head.

"I really need to find a new place to live." Twisting around, Madison quickly switched hands on the pipe, gasping when another spurt of water shot into her face.

With his hands braced against the door facing, Jonah

made a leisurely survey of the scene. "Or you could try taking a shower the way the rest of us do—inside the stall." Dressed in a pair of low hanging pajama pants that exposed a long, lean torso and those well-defined, V-shaped lats that attracted women in droves, Jonah gave her a crooked grin. His gaze skimmed over Madison's water-spattered glasses, then drifted downward, lingering on her thin nightshirt. Madison followed the direction of his glance and noticed that her nightshirt had been transformed into a prize-winning wet T-shirt after being hosed down by the broken water pipe.

"Seriously, Jonah, I need to get a better place."

Jonah cleared his throat. "Ah, you should probably get changed first," he teased.

"And you've got ten seconds to move," she warned, her teeth chattering as she repositioned her grip, ready to aim the spray Jonah's way. "Otherwise, you're next."

"Right. I'm on it." He disappeared from the doorway and hurried down the steep steps. A loud clang and few curses later, the gushing water trickled to a drip before coming to a full stop. Madison stepped back, wiped the moisture from her glasses, and attempted to squeeze the droplets from her long, soggy hair.

The old floorboards creaked under Jonah's weight as he jogged back to the bathroom. He grabbed a big, fluffy towel from the hook on the door and tossed it her way. Keeping his bare feet out of the ever-expanding puddle, he stood in the hall and braced his hands on the overhead door frame.

He assessed the damage and pulled a disgruntled face, one that made him look young and more boyish than his twenty-five years and had her thoughts careening back to their playground days.

One eyebrow arched when he asked, "You want me to call or do you want to?"

Madison pressed the towel to her chest and blotted her

cold cheeks with a corner, groaning as she fought off a sneeze. She was battling the summer cold of the century—during Austin's worst heat wave, nonetheless—and really wasn't in the mood to get into another shouting match with her land-lord. Besides, she already knew how the scenario would play out. Over the phone he'd promise to come by right away, going so far as to ensure her he was practically on her front stoop. Past experiences, however, had taught her that he'd show up on her doorstep at his leisure, leaving her high and dry, or in this case, wet and sodden, for days on end.

"You'd better do it this time." She grabbed a couple of towels from the sliver of a linen closet and tossed them onto the flooded tile floor before adding, "Not that I think it will do any good."

Jonah tapped his fingers on the paint-chipped doorframe and nodded in agreement. "Maybe I should just call Brad. He'll know what to do."

At the mention of Jonah's older brother, a shiver moved through Madison, one that had little to do with the water chilling her feverish skin and everything to do with the hot hunk of military man who had been invading her dreams since her teen years.

"What would I know how to do?"

Jonah spun around. "Hey, bro. Just in time."

"What would I know?" Brad began again, but his words fell off. Madison glanced up, expecting to see him surveying the bathroom, only to find him looking directly at her breasts and the ample curves she spent years hiding. Her nipples tightened in response, unbridled desire moving into her quiv-ering stomach as their gazes collided.

"We...uh...we had another flood," she managed to croak out, hoping she didn't sound as breathless as she felt.

"I can see that," he responded, his voice sounding tighter than normal.

Her blood pulsed hot when his smoldering gaze tracked a path down her body—a slow, lazy caress that instantly pushed back the cold inside her. Heat bombarded her as she became fully aware of her near-naked state—fully aware of what else Brad could *see*.

She snatched another towel from the closet and let it drop down in front of her as his gaze tracked back up her body and met hers. For a moment, she could almost swear there had been a flicker of interest backlighting his baby blues, but he gave a quick shake of his head and tore his gaze from hers. When he frowned and took in the sad state of her century-old bathroom, she knew she had to be mistaken. Guys like Brad didn't lust after girls like her. No, he was into vivacious, self-assured women. Brazen women who had it all and weren't afraid to use it to get what they wanted.

What he wasn't into were girls who spent the better part of their lives being called Fatty Maddy, along with a few other unkind names like S'mores Cracker.

Madison wrapped the towel around her chest and tucked it in, then reached for another to blot the water from her hair. It wasn't that she was fat, per se. She had been an early bloomer and had body image issues. She had worn oversized, bulky layers of clothing to cover her D-cup breasts and curvy hips, but rather than camouflaging her full figure, she had ended up looking like a big, round marshmallow. Sort of like a female version of the Michelin Man. That, of course, coupled with the last name Graham, was how the mean girls—and boys—from high school came up with the S'mores dig. God, teenagers really were the cruelest beings on earth—and, as far as she was concerned, not all that creative, either.

Size twelve boots splashed in the water as Brad stepped into the tight confines of the bathroom. Her pulse jumped in her throat as he leaned past her to look at the broken pipe. She tried to breathe in his familiar scent of fresh soap and clean skin, but her stuffed-up nose took that moment to run, gushing with the same enthusiasm as her broken pipe. Damn. She quickly reached for her box of tissue, only to find that it had become a casualty of faulty plumbing as well. In a very unattractive, unladylike move she sniffed hard, and, because the fate-Gods liked to kick her when she was down, Brad took that moment straighten to his full height and look directly at her.

Okay, her day had officially gone from bad to worse.

"Grab my toolbox from the truck," he said to Jonah, and that's when she realized he sounded as hoarse as she did, and that he was likely battling a cold too.

He folded his arms over his chest, the soft fabric of his T-shirt stretching across his broad shoulders. He took his time to inspect the damage, pulling the same disgruntled face that Jonah had earlier. Only on Brad, the expression was anything but boyish. Oh no, not at all. Here stood a *man*, ready to take charge, to do whatever was necessary to get the job done, and take all the time he needed to do it. A man who wasn't afraid to roll up his sleeves and get his hands dirty...or wet. It made him look hot and sexy and—good God, she needed to pull herself together!

Clearing her throat, Madison turned her thoughts to the two men in her life. Even though there was only two years between them, at twenty-seven, Brad was all man. One hundred percent grade-A male. The kind she wanted to serve up on a shiny platter and dive into with vigor. Hunger moved through her and she worked to find her voice as she finger combed her hair in some feeble attempt to make herself look presentable.

He shot a quick glance her way and a strange look came over his face, one she couldn't quite identify. "You...uh...you might want to get out of those wet clothes before you catch your death of cold." His turn of phrase reminded her of his late folks, his dad in particular.

"I've already got a cold," she mumbled, stepping onto one of the soaked towels. She pulled open the vanity drawer, grabbed her trusty lip balm, and applied it to her chapped lip. As the scent of cherry filled the air, she caught Brad wetting his own mouth, like he too was in need of relief.

"Want some?" She held the tube out to him. "It's cherry flavor, but it works."

His gaze dropped to her mouth, and then quickly darted away. "No," he bit out, his harsh tone surprising her.

She recapped the tube and tossed it back into her vanity. "What, you don't like cherry?"

The muscles along his jaw rippled. "I never said that."

Jonah came back with Brad's toolbox and she let the matter drop. Jonah stepped up beside his brother, and Madison smacked her lips to spread the balm. She couldn't help but compare the two men as they stood side by side. Where Brad was taller, with harder muscles and sharper features, Jonah was lean with a pretty-boy face. With his angelic attributes, Jonah would look at home on any Calvin Klein poster, although Madison couldn't help but wonder what his older brother would look like in those sexy designer underwear.

Along with his boyish good looks, Jonah was also easygoing, the life of the party and game for just about anything. Brad, on the other hand, was far more responsible. When his dad had died of lung disease after a long hard battle, and his mother shortly after, ovarian cancer taking her out quickly, Brad had stepped into a parental role, despite the fact that he was only a teen himself. He always looked out for his reckless kid brother, and was a real hands-on kind of guy, in the field as an explosive expert and around the house as a handyman.

Speaking of hands on...

Her gaze moved to his hands as he searched through his toolbox. He picked up a wrench, looked it over, then carefully put it back and chose another. As she thought about how meticulous he was in everything he did, her brain took a brief, luxurious moment to think about what those rough palms of his would feel like on her flesh. She imagined he was a considerate lover, and that his touches would be slow, thorough and needy, his kisses hot and demanding as he trailed a path downward, his tongue moving closer and closer to the warm juncture between her legs, to the greedy little spot that needed him the most.

"...Madison."

The sound of Brad's voice brought her thoughts crashing back to reality. She took in his watchful eyes and wondered what he'd just said to her. "Ummm," she murmured, blinking rapidly. "What was that again?"

Before Brad could answer, Jonah stepped up to her. "Are you okay?" His brows pulled into a thoughtful frown as he reached out and pressed the backs of his fingers to her forehead. "Jesus, you're burning up."

Oh God, he had no idea.

"I'm fine," she assured him and squared her shoulders. "It's just really hot in here."

She seriously needed to get it together before she threw herself at Brad and begged him to take her—right there on the wet bathroom floor. Not that Brad thought of her in a sexual way, or that she'd actually have the nerve to bare herself to him. No, that was never going to happen. Even if by some miracle Madison had the opportunity to get between the sheets with him, it was a pretty sure bet she'd run the other way, because she had a feeling Brad was the kind of guy who'd want to make love with the lights on, and take his good old time exploring his woman's body. Her skin tightened, and a strange, strangled noise caught in her throat as she imagined his attention focused on her body—his hands and eyes moving over her, touching her, seeing her. All of her.

Okay, okay, so there was no denying that she still had body image issues, and was just as insecure today as she was all those years ago. She cupped the towel against her chest tighter and darted a quick glance Brad's way.

His nostrils flared as he massaged his temples with his thumb and forefinger. "Go get changed. Now."

"Oh, right."

Adjusting the towel so it dipped in the back, making sure her backside was covered, Madison stepped past Brad and splashed her way down the hall. She could hear him digging around in his toolbox as she made a beeline to her bedroom. Once inside she shut the door and sagged against it, her libidinous body still feeling the effects of Brad's close proximity and rugged good looks. A breeze drifted in from her open window, the morning air cooling her damp body and helping to focus her thoughts.

With the gust of air giving her a burst of energy after a sleepless night, she peeled off her wet T-shirt and glanced at her clock, wondering what Brad was doing at her place so early in the morning. She tugged on her work scrubs and grabbed a clean apron from the laundry basket, then stopped dead in her tracks. Without water, she wouldn't be able to open her bakery, and if she couldn't open her doors, she'd never make enough money to find a decent place to live. Damn, damn, damn.

With so much to do today she could only hope that Brad could get the plumbing fixed right away. She took a breath to collect her thoughts, then made a mental list of everything she had to do. As soon as her assistant, and other childhood best friend, Sophie Edwards, arrived Sophie could go to work on serving the breakfast crowd—providing they had water— while Madison darted to the country club to showcase cake samples to a bridal party. Once she got that out of the way she could get a start on making the truckload of cupcakes she'd promised to donate to the city's upcoming Fourth of July festival. The school band was counting on her donations to help raise funds for their fall trip and she didn't want to let them down.

The sound of a car pulling into the back parking lot behind the shop signaled Sophie's arrival for her shift, but if Madison couldn't open for the day, she'd have to turn her around and send her right back home. Not that she thought Sophie would mind. Working at the café and taking summer classes at night was no easy feat, and with her exams coming up, she could likely use the extra hours to study.

Smoothing her hair down and wishing the pipe had broken *after* she had showered, Madison adjusted her glasses, knotted her apron around her waist and made her way back to the brothers.

"Any luck?" she asked hopefully.

Jonah shook his head and wrung out another wet towel over the tub. "Brad doesn't have the right parts."

Her glance shot to Brad, who was down on his knees, and she swallowed hard, because from where she stood, it was abundantly clear that Brad had *all* the right parts. Then he turned his head and coughed into the crook of his arm and guilt ate at Madison.

The man was sick and the last thing he needed was to be ankle deep in icy water. This was her rental house, her mess, and she should be the one fixing it, not him.

Madison frowned. She knew what she had to do, even though she couldn't afford it. "It's okay, Brad. I'm going to call a plumber."

Brad stood and blue eyes that mirrored his brother's latched on to hers. "I can fix this for you, Madison. It's just a matter of getting the right supplies. I can do that after I drop Jonah off."

Jonah ran his hands through his short, cropped hair and looked at his watch. "Shit, I'm running late. I'll grab my gear." He cast his brother a glance. "Mind if I take a quick shower at your place before we go?"

Brad nodded and Madison stepped to the side to let her roommate push past her. With all the commotion and the brain fog from her cold, she'd forgotten that it was the first of the month and Jonah was leaving on a job this morning.

After finishing their tour in Afghanistan, both Jonah and Brad had decided to expound on their military experience and returned home to do contract bomb hunting here on American soil, defusing munitions that had been left over from former training camps during the wars. Today was Jonah's day to leave on a convoy, heading north for the next month to search for and defuse old bombs. Which, of course, accounted for why his brother had shown up at her place so early. He was here to drive Jonah to the departure site some twenty miles outside of town.

Contracting out as explosive experts was their main line of work, but when they weren't away they could be found at the old abandoned base training service dogs with their fellow comrades. With Brad's love of restoring things, he could also be found helping out in their friend's motorcycle shop, or working on the old Victorian house left to him by his ailing grandfather.

Brad tossed his gear back into his toolbox, then stood, his body crowding hers in the confided space.

When he coughed again, she said, "Brad you don't have to do this. You're not feeling well."

"Neither are you, which is why I need to get this done right away. You won't get a plumber in here for hours, and I don't want you without water for that long."

Her heart tightened at his thoughtfulness but before she could respond, she heard Sophie's voice at the foot of the stairs. "Hey, Madison, what's going on?"

"Come on up and see for yourself," Madison called out. She stepped into the hall to meet her friend, and when Sophie took one look at her hair, she crinkled her nose.

"Did you get in a fight with the egg beater?"

Great, just what she needed, her friend drawing attention to her frazzled hair. As if a red, stuffed-up nose and watery eyes weren't bad enough. Madison pulled an elastic band off her wrist and tied back her long, wet curls. "Broken pipe."

"Again?" Sophie groaned when she reached the landing.

"Yeah, because it was never fixed right in the first place," Brad's deep voice rumbled from within the bathroom.

Sophie stepped past Madison, and her eyes lit up when she spotted Brad. "Hey, Brad," she said in the same flirtatious tone she always used around the Crosby brothers. Her gaze rolled over him and Madison worked to smother a spark of jealousy she knew better than to feel. "I didn't realize you were back."

"Been back for a while now."

Surprised to hear that, Madison's head came back with a start. She hadn't seen Brad around for weeks and just assumed he was hanging out in Tallulah, Louisiana, after his friend's wedding. No doubt he'd found himself a nice, hot bridesmaid to occupy himself with.

Come to think of it, Brad had been coming around her place less and less and it made her wonder if the brothers had had a fight, although Jonah hadn't mentioned anything about it.

"So, how was the wedding?" Sophie asked.

His grin was wry, highly sardonic. "Let's just say it's good to be home." The look on his face combined with his dark tone let them both know how he felt about love and marriage. Unlike his brother, who loved to play the field and had no desire to change his lifestyle, Brad hadn't always hated the idea of settling down. In fact, he'd been engaged once himself. But it had turned out badly when he'd come back from his tour early to find his girl in bed with another guy— or at least that's what Madison had heard. He'd changed after that, dating casually, avoiding commitment, and rarely staying in one place for very long.

"Why don't you grab your stuff—" Brad gestured past Madison's shoulder, nodding toward her bedroom, "—and you can shower at my place while I drop Jonah off and make a quick trip to the hardware store."

The thought of climbing into his shower, using the same soap he'd lathered his body with earlier that morning had her nipples aching and her sex moistening. Hoping to hide her body's reaction, she coughed into her sleeve and said, "That's okay, I can just grab a shower at Sophie's."

"Only if you're really, really quiet." Sophie frowned and smoothed her blonde hair behind her ears. "Karley was up with the baby all night and the two are sleeping it off."

Madison drove her hands into her apron pockets. She'd forgotten that their friend Karley and her newborn Brooklyn were staying with Sophie until her husband returned from overseas.

"Besides," Brad said, "you don't want to spread your cold germs around."

It was true. She didn't want to risk giving her germs to an infant.

"Yeah," Sophie agreed, her expression deadpan as she nudged Madison with her elbow. "You should probably go to Brad's. That way you can make as much noise as you want. Heck, you could even scream and no one would hear you."

Fully aware of her friend's innuendo, Madison sniffed and glared at her. Oh, she was so going to kill her when she got her alone. "But then I'll be spreading my germs around his place, won't I?"

As if on cue Brad sneezed. "I've got a cold too, so it won't matter." Madison exhaled slowly, grateful that he hadn't picked up on Sophie's sexual innuendo. Giving her no time to protest, Brad slipped past them. "I'll meet you at the truck."

When he disappeared down the steps, Jonah came out from his room looking rugged and handsome dressed in his army fatigues. "Hey, Sophie," he greeted before turning to Madison. "Dibs on the first shower," he said, in typical Jonah fashion, then rushed down the steps after his brother.

A wide grin split Sophie's face as she watched him go, her gaze latched on his backside until he disappeared outside. "So," she said, "you live with one of the hottest guys I know and are about to shower at his gorgeous brother's place." Sophie tapped a painted nail on her pursed lips and Madison could almost hear the wheels turning when a sound of delight rumbled in her friend's throat. "Forget S'mores Cracker, girl-friend. I think it's high time you made yourself a *Graham Sandwich*, don't you?"

———

Jesus Christ, Madison was going to be the death of him.

He'd been hoping to avoid her when he showed up to collect his brother, and the last thing he expected was to find her in a goddamn wet T-shirt, looking so fucking hot he almost shot off a load then and there.

Brad drummed his fingers on his steering wheel and shifted in his seat, uncomfortable as his cock pressed insis-tently against his unforgiving jeans. Christ, seeing her in that T-shirt, blinking up at him with those dark bedroom eyes of hers as the lush swell of her body beckoned his touch—his cock—had damn near done him in.

Fuck.

He'd be lying if he said he didn't want her in his bed. Every time he looked at her all he could think about was caging her beneath him and fucking her long and hard, driving balls deep until she screamed out his name. Oh yeah, he'd make her scream, and when he did—contrary to what Sophie thought—*everyone* would hear it.

Maybe then he'd be able to stop thinking about her when he was alone at night. Hell, who was he kidding? He thought about her even when he wasn't alone.

He'd always liked his kid brother's best friend, but six months ago, after returning home from a long overseas tour, he suddenly began to see the sweet girl next door in different ways.

Sinful ways...

But he wasn't going to act on his urges, not when she had something going on with Jonah. Shit...

Truthfully, Brad wasn't sure what kind of relationship the two had, considering he'd seen them both date other people over the years. But from the comfort level between them, to the way they took care of each other, even going so far as to sharing a place when Jonah had finished his last tour, he knew there had to be deeper feelings involved, and he wasn't about to take her to his bed, no matter how much he wanted her naked and beneath him. Or naked and on top.

Or just plain naked.

Jonah tossed his rucksack into the truck bed and slid into the cab, pulling Brad's thoughts back from fantasyland. "Hey, bro, what's up?"

Brad put his key into the ignition and turned the engine over. "Nothing." He clenched his jaw hard as he watched Madison and Sophie exit from the downstairs bakery. A frown marred Madison's pretty face as she spoke to her friend, the

Sweetie's Bakery *Closed* sign on the door behind her rattling against the glass pane as she locked up. Brad gripped the steering wheel harder. He hated seeing her living and working in such a shitty place, and he knew today's loss of income was going to have a serious effect on her bank account.

"You have that look on your face again."

Brad angled his head toward his brother. "What look is that?"

Jonah grinned. "The one you get just before you kick the shit out of me."

Brad glared at his brother and scoffed. "Evidently, I should have beaten you more often." Okay, so he might have roughed up his punk-ass brother a time or two over the years, but it was only because Jonah had needed it. The boy was a damn fool sometimes, getting into messes that Brad had to clean up behind him.

"Yeah, well, that's a matter of opinion," Jonah said.

He held his brother's gaze. "You got something to say?"

Jonah held his hands up and laughed. "Nope."

Madison tapped on the window and Jonah jumped onto the sidewalk to let her climb into the middle. Without conscious thought Brad's eyes roamed the sexy curves she always kept hidden behind those baggy clothes and icing-stained apron. Damned if he didn't want to peel those loose-fitting work clothes from her body so he could touch and kiss her lush contours until she writhed beneath him and cried out his name.

As Madison slid in beside him, her duffle bag clutched to her chest, want pumped through his veins, the sudden, urgent need to help himself to a taste of her sweetness pulling at him hard. Fuck. He looked away, staring at some random woman walking her dog while he did his damnedest to ignore his raging hard-on.

"Here, give me that." Jonah took the bag from her and tossed it into the truck bed with his.

Once he jumped back into the cab, Brad put the vehicle into gear, turned his attention to the road ahead and slipped into traffic. Jonah punched up the volume on the radio and hooked his left arm over the back of the seat, pulling Madison toward him.

Brad tried to focus on his driving, he really did, but with Madison's leg rubbing up against his it took effort to stay on the road.

He drove through the downtown core, and when they passed a vacant building, a *For Sale* sign on the window, Jonah turned to Madison. "Maybe when I get back we can look for a new place to live."

She looked at the building, and there was a hint of gloom in her voice when she said, "I can't afford to rent an apart-ment *and* a business front, and it won't be easy to find a place where I can live upstairs and turn the main level into Sweetie's."

Jonah curved his arm around her and pulled her in closer. As she rested her head on his shoulder, he brushed a light kiss over her hair. "Don't worry. I'll be making some good coin out on the road. It'll go a long way in finding something nicer than we have now."

Feeling like a third wheel, an eavesdropper listening in on a private, intimate conversation, Brad cast a glance their way. His gut clenched when he saw Madison smile up at Jonah. Hell, the two of them even talked like an old married couple. There was no missing how much his brother cared for her, which only solidified Brad's vow to keep his distance where Madison was concerned.

Of course, she wasn't the first girl Brad had walked away from because of his brother. Jonah was fun, wild and had a reputation with the ladies. As teens, a few of Brad's girlfriends had gravitated toward his charismatic younger brother. Even though Brad wanted to beat the shit out of Jonah for taking his girl instead of doing the honorable thing and backing off, Brad always walked away. Blood was blood and no way would he allow a girl to come between him and his brother. How much could any of those girls have cared anyway, if they had no trouble leaving one brother for the other? Besides, he'd promised his dad that he'd take care of Jonah, and as a man of his word, he chose his family battles carefully. As long as Jonah treated the women properly, there'd be no trouble between brothers.

His thoughts careened back to a couple years ago, to the night he found his fiancée Jocelyn in bed with another man—doing the one thing he wouldn't dream of asking her to do for him, considering she'd blatantly told him oral sex was disgusting and there wasn't a girl in the world who enjoyed giving it. Although she enjoyed the hell out of it when he'd gone down on her, which he did frequently. Fuck, he wasn't sure what hurt more, seeing her mouth wrapped around some douchebag's cock, or realizing how stupid she thought he was when she starting spilling lies, telling him it wasn't what he thought. Sure, whatever. Wouldn't be the first time a woman had fallen and landed with a hard-on in her mouth and a pair of balls in her hand. Oh yeah, shit like that happened all the time.

He could have stayed and fought for her, but any girl who would sleep with another man and lie about it while her fiancé was overseas fighting for their country wasn't worth the battle. And after seeing the same thing happen to a few of his comrades, he'd come to learn that long-distance relationships never worked. Since Brad's work continued to take him out of state, he decided never to get himself in that kind of situation again. No, now he was into casual sex, no commitments.

"Besides," Jonah said, "Brad can help us turn any space into a bakery. Right, bro?"

"Yeah, sure." Brad looked at Madison, and when she turned her bright-eyed smile his way, his heart nearly stopped.

She ran paint-chipped nails along the deep hollow of her throat, and as he watched the movement his mouth watered, his tongue wanting to follow the path of her hands. Heat throbbed through him, and his cock thickened once again, aching to pound into her, hard hot strokes that would leave them both sated and breathless and would finally, *finally*, get her out of his head.

"And if something else goes wrong with the place while I'm away, Brad's your man," Jonah said.

As Brad pictured himself stepping in for his brother, his mind ran wild with one delicious idea after the other, and he forced himself to cough, hoping it would rattle some sense back into his lust-drunk brain.

"Isn't that right, Brad?"

"Yeah." He nodded. "I can help you out with anything you need."

Something flitted across her face when she asked, "Anything?"

"Yeah, anything," he assured her, but when she drew her bottom lip between her teeth, and her eyes glazed over like she had other things on her mind, he wondered if they were still talking about her run-down rental...or something else entirely.

ABOUT CATHRYN

New York Times and *USA today* Bestselling author, Cathryn is a wife, mom, sister, daughter, and friend. She loves dogs, sunny weather, anything chocolate (she never says no to a brownie) pizza and red wine. She has two teenagers who keep her busy with their never ending activities, and a husband who is convinced he can turn her into a mixed martial arts fan. Cathryn can never find balance in her life, is always trying to find time to go to the gym, can never keep up with emails, Facebook or Twitter and tries to write page-turning books that her readers will love.

Connect with Cathryn:
Newsletter
https://app.mailerlite.com/webforms/landing/c1f8n1
Twitter: https://twitter.com/writercatfox
Facebook:
https://www.facebook.com/AuthorCathrynFox?ref=hl
Blog: http://cathrynfox.com/blog/
Goodreads:
https://www.goodreads.com/author/show/91799.Cathryn_Fox

Pinterest http://www.pinterest.com/catkalen/

ALSO BY CATHRYN FOX

Players on Ice
The Playmaker
The Stick Handler
The Body Checker
The Hard Hitter

In the Line of Duty
His Obsession Next Door
His Strings to Pull
His Trouble in Talulah
His Taste of Temptation
His Moment to Steal
His Best Friend's Girl
His Reason to Stay

Confessions
Confessions of a Bad Boy Professor
Confessions of a Bad Boy Officer
Confessions of a Bad Boy Fighter
Confessions of a Bad Boy Gamer
Confessions of a Bad Boy Millionaire
Confessions of a Bad Boy Santa
Confessions of a Bad Boy CEO

Hands On

Hands On

Body Contact

Full Exposure

Dossier

Private Reserve

House Rules

Under Pressure

Big Catch

Brazilian Fantasy

Improper Proposal

Boys of Beachville

Good at Being Bad

Igniting the Bad Boy

Bad Girl Therapy

Stone Cliff Series:

Crashing Down

Wasted Summer

Love Lessons

Wrapped Up

Eternal Pleasure Series

Instinctive

Impulsive

Indulgent

Sun Stroked Series

Seaside Seduction

Deep Desire

Private Pleasure

Captured and Claimed Series:

Yours to Take

Yours to Teach

Yours to Keep

Firefighter Heat Series

Fever

Siren

Flash Fire

Playing For Keeps Series

Slow Ride

Wild Ride

Sweet Ride

Breaking the Rules:

Hold Me Down Hard

Pin Me Up Proper

Tie Me Down Tight

Stand Alone Title:

Hands on with the CEO

Torn Between Two Brothers

Holiday Spirit

Unleashed

Knocking on Demon's Door

Web of Desire

www.ingramcontent.com/pod-product-compliance
Lightning Source LLC
Chambersburg PA
CBHW050402190726

48284CB00007BB/2398